RAINBOW CHILD

RAINBOW CHILD

Through The Eyes of a Young Girl,

We See Ourselves

S L COYNE

Rainbow Child

S.L.Coyne © 2014
All rights reserved

A record of this publication is available from
the British Library.

ISBN 978-1-907203-92-3

Typesetting by Wordzworth Ltd
www.wordzworth.com

Cover design by Titanium Design Ltd
www.titaniumdesign.co.uk

Printed by Lightning Source UK
www.lightningsource.com

Cover image by *www.freefever.com*, with thanks

**LOCAL
LEGEND**

Published by Local Legend
www.local-legend.co.uk

ABOUT THE AUTHOR

Born in Wiltshire, England, of Irish parents, S L Coyne grew up in a family of chefs, musicians and singers. Her earliest ambition was to be an ice skater, for which she trained professionally until a cliff fall put an end to her dream.

She has an Honours degree in Religious Studies and has travelled extensively, studying screenwriting at the University of California, Berkeley, and Montessori education in Italy, before returning to live in London. She has now been teaching for more than twenty years, specialising in Special Needs education, and has published several poems and short stories.

Rainbow Child is her brilliant debut novel. Beautifully written in language that is alternately lyrical and childlike, it is the story of young Rebekah and the people she discovers as her family settle in a new town far from their familiar home. As dark secrets begin to unravel, her life takes many turns both delightful and terrifying as the story builds to a tragic and breathless climax that just keeps on going.

This is a story of how we see others who are 'different'. Through the eyes of Rebekah, writing equally with passion and humour, we see the truth of human nature...

—ONE—

Lightning and crashing thunder stops the world in a breath while I wait for the onslaught. A scratch of light through a blackened sky and there in front of me is a multi-coloured arch. The rainbow beams across the dark skies where shadow likes to dwell.

Another flash of light and I remember nothing. I only see rainbows of colour with such beauty and fluid grace. Red, orange fused with yellow melting into green that pours itself into blue. And there in the blue dances the shadow that yawns and stretches itself into indigo and becomes an echo within the violet.

Tiny prisms of water disperse light and blessings into a multicoloured ribbon of forgiveness. The dancing colours streaming across the sky are a reminder of a Near Life Experience, that my life before was but a dream. I was seven when it happened to me and my life changed in so many ways. I developed an illness that left invisible scars. As I grew up, I realised what exactly I had been left with.

When the years of growing up had gone by and I was so-called mature enough to look back on my childhood, I shudder at the incident that happened and the events leading up to it. I would say that it all started with me trying to rescue Megan from the dock, but the shadow said it had started long before. The shadow told me it had begun when we moved to a certain town and that somehow the shock had contributed to me developing the illness...

This particular town was unpretentious yet enough for me to despise its very name. It was small, sandwiched between the sea and empty hills. Before one reached the town, the tall chimneys of squashed factories stood like gates heralding the doom, spewing their contents into the sky until heavenly clouds mingled with the nebulae of men's greed. The clouds were blown slowly across the sky out towards the sea - over the town, a town of ignorance and secrets trapped behind square walls of red brick and grey roofs. A small town!

Being of Irish descent, it was a source of honour to some members of the family that we had recorded ancestors dating back to the beginning of time. Well, maybe that's an exaggeration though the family name was first recorded in Connacht and Leinster, and as leaders of our province we ruled happily until the King of Leinster got greedy. Many proud native Irish families lost everything. Then in 1845 the great potato famine caused widespread poverty and the exodus from Ireland began.

Many joined the armada of sailing ships for the New World. The romantics, or bullshitters as Uncle Danny referred to them, called these ships 'white sails'. The realists like my father called them 'the coffin ships' as many of the passengers died of disease and the elements. My great-grandfather Joseph embarked for England and a particular fishing town that slowly grew to become one of the biggest fishing ports in the world. With hard work, determination and a good helping of double dealing, Joseph became rich and was able to buy a fleet of trawlers before he reached his mid-twenties.

But great-grandfather felt a yearning for his home country and bought a huge derelict mansion in the south-west of Ireland with hopes of filling it with a family of strong sons. After tasting the delights of every other woman in town, he discovered a wife and eventually had six daughters and one son, much to his displeasure. His gambling only surpassed by his drinking, he then died before he was forty, leaving great-grandma with seven children and a business. She struggled on and dedicated most, if not all, of her time to the business, neglecting her children in the process. Thus my grand-father grew up without love and so was never able to show emotion to my father, who in turn could never show it to my older brother Peter and my sister Leah, nearly five years older than me.

However, my father did treat me differently, perhaps taking pity on me being the youngest. Though his apparently calm and unruf-fled exterior gave no hint of how he really felt towards any of his children, he channeled a great deal of intense emotional energy into the care and control of us. Unfortunately, control was the operative word for Peter and Leah, while he could be surprisingly gentle when confronted with a timid and frightened child such as me.

Father was a fisherman, like all the men in our family, and had secured a house in that small English town on one of his fishing trips. Mother sorted and packed everything and at last the car was finally loaded up and we began our long journey to the place that would change all our lives. It was about three in the morning when we finally arrived and even then a particular house held a certain fascination for me. Peter woke me up just as we turned into our new street.

"Wake up squirt, we've arrived."

"Welcome to Hell," murmured Leah.

I stretched my legs and half opened my eyes to see a tall, decrepit house dominating the street where we would live. Its eyes surveyed the avenue. It knew everything that was going on.

The car pulled into the kerb and stopped outside a white house that was joined onto others. I hadn't seen anything like this except in the town near Beaulieu, the family home in Ireland. We stumbled out of the car and opened the gate; mother had the keys, she opened the front door and we lumbered up the stairs, found a bedroom with a bed and just collapsed onto it. We would argue about whose bed it would be tomorrow. Leah and Peter lay on either side and I plopped down in between them. We could hear mother and father bringing the luggage in, then the familiar sound of father's black bag being dumped near the front door. We heard mother say:

"So, nothing's gonna change here either, eh?"

"I have to work."

"Aye, that's always your excuse, isn't it?"

"Well, give me a reason not to leave so often."

"You'll be waiting a long time."

"Aye, nothing changes, does it, dear?"

Peter rolled over onto his side and curled himself into a ball while Leah got up and shut the door. Our parents' coldness to one another drifted up the stairs and mingled with the cold breeze that came from the street, finding its way into a bedroom of three tired children.

It was a rough old town but it felt new to me as it was completely different to anything I had known before. The people seemed to ignore you but then perhaps they didn't know who I was. Yet everyone in the town knew our name.

Little big English town had strange kind of weather, to say the least. In the summertime, when the sun did eventually break through the clouds, it was so hot you couldn't bear to be out in it. And the factories sent their perpetual clouds over us so you could taste the chemicals in your mouth and an odour of dull, dirty pollution clung to your clothes. Come to think of it, that's probably why people walked round with long faces and never smiled at others passing by.

The people moved quickly, pushing and shoving and never caring, it seemed. They never concerned themselves with other people.

Children and parents were of the same breed, never knowing or even attempting to understand one another. Parents worked and children went to school. Then you returned home, cooked the meal, cleared the table, washed the dishes, gave the children a bath, got them to bed and said goodnight. Parents only saw their children for half an hour in the morning, yet when the evening came round they could not wait to send them to bed. Life went on like this, never stopping. The wheels never ceased turning.

We lived in a house that was in a row of terraced houses with red roofs, in the middle of the town near the prosperous shopping centre yet also in walking distance of the poor shopping centre. Little big town had a mixture of very rich people and extremely poor people. Everything seemed to be near everything. The houses were near the shops, which were near the school. Our local shop was strategically placed between school and home. It sold newspapers, groceries, bits and bobs, amazing sweets in different jars, sweets in different colours, shapes and sizes. Mr McEnfry sold everything imaginable and his shop was never empty. He was open all the time, morning, noon and night. I don't think he ever slept. I liked living in that neighbourhood and for a time it seemed to like me.

So we lived at one hundred and twenty-two, Margaret Avenue. Mother was not happy to be living in a terraced house but my father had decided it would be better if we lived in the town so the children would be close to their friends; in the country we would only have ourselves for company and that would be disastrous for me. Peter and Leah were older than me and never really wanted to play any games.

Mother was as smooth as silk on one side and jagged as razors on the other. She seemed to be in a perpetual state of menopause. She had been going through the menopause since having me at twenty-eight and every time she saw me I reminded her of how bad she felt. On the odd occasion that she played with me, being such a lively and spontaneous person she left me way behind, playing with zest and enthusiasm until she lost interest. She did not have the patience for a clinging child who demands endless cuddles.

I got along with my father but he was seldom home, going away for weeks on end on fishing trips. I soon realised it was better to leave the house and wander around the local neighbourhood and it was on one of these adventures that I met Megan and the friends.

After slamming the front door in a fit of rebellion, which I immediately regretted though could do nothing about, I proceeded to walk down the street. At one end there were a couple of girls playing and at the other end I could just make out a figure sitting on a wall. I decided to walk towards the figure as I thought it looked safe enough. She was rather taller than me and a little bit better built. She wore glasses and had long red hair tied into two big bunches that stuck out, each bunch with a big green bow in it. The green bow matched her green dress. She wore white ankle socks which had frogs on them - I figured she liked green. However, her shoes were black with little green bows stuck on.

I stopped walking and looked at her, not too sure whether I should speak or do as mother had always ordered, 'Never speak until you're spoken to'. While pondering this, the figure caught me looking at her and spoke.

"Ello!" it said.

I was dumbfounded she would want to speak to me so I stood still, looking on.

"Ello!" it said again.

This time I prompted myself to speak. "Hello," I muttered.

"Ello!" said the voice for a third time.

"Hello," I replied properly this time and I waited to see what the figure would do or say next.

"My n… name is… is… Me… Megan!" And she pointed to herself.

"Oh," I muttered, wondering why she had to remind herself she was there. I also wondered about the way she talked, alternately shouting and giggling.

"Wh… Wh… What's yourrr n… name?"

Yep, Megan was definitely strange, but something about her put me at ease so I replied, "My name's Becky and I've just moved in down the street." I pointed to the house.

"I ha… ha… have been he… here long t… ti… time," Megan said, nodding her head.

Before I had the chance to say anything else, a woman - I presumed it was her mother - came out the house. She was dressed in a smart, dark blue suit and wore a hat of the same colour which had a big bow at the back; she came charging out the house as if she were going to war with someone. I was soon to find out whom.

"Look here, you," she said, pointing her finger at me. "How many times do I have to tell you to leave my daughter alone? She doesn't want to play with people who call her names."

I stood on in innocent wonder.

"Come along, Megan," she said softly to her daughter. "We'll be late for church."

Megan jumped down off the wall and her hand automatically folded into her mother's. Then she began to skip away with her mother who turned to me with expectant eyes. I was too dumbstruck to say anything. I stared after them as they marched off and knew which one was giving the orders. Megan had ceased to skip.

Meanwhile the girls at the end of the street had heard all the commotion and had decided to see what it was all about. As I turned round there was a girl the same height as me and, I assumed, the same age. In between chewing on some gum, and with one hand on her hip, she inquired, "So what was all the fuss about, then?"

"I don't know," I shrugged my shoulders. "I was just talking to Megan."

"Yuk! You was talking to Dumbo?" said another girl.

"Dumbo Jumbo," another joined in, after which they all started giggling.

"Why do you call her that?"

"Because she's divvy. She has to go to a special school now."

"Special school," repeated another girl, nodding her head.

I examined the three hoodlums, thought of Megan's mother and understood what she'd meant. Furthermore, I realised I would be better off with Megan's mother than these three. They left me in the middle of Empty Street after asking if I wanted to hang out with them. They got bored waiting for me to answer and I watched them flick their hair and strut away like peacocks.

A sharp breeze slapped me awake. I turned round to where Megan had been sitting. Then I noticed it, the house I remembered from the night we came here. It was a huge, grey derelict house that seemed to dominate the whole avenue. I drifted closer to it. The house had seen me. The gate was off its hinges, the garden was wild and the grass made an imitation of a hedge. At either side there were two huge trees and as I stepped into their shadows it felt like paddling in an icy pond. I breathed in the stillness of it all. The grand strangeness enhanced my guilt that I had not acknowledged this house before; it was a temple where I should bow my head in gratitude.

A hand bounced on my shoulder, startling me, and I jumped round. They were gathered near me again. With a hand pointing at the house and the other twiddling her Rapunzel locks, she spoke to me.

"Look, as you're new here I might as well give you a lesson or two."

I glanced round. The smallest of the three stood furthest away and the other fairytale child stood beside me with her arms folded.

"That place is 'aunted."

"Haunted. What do you mean?"

"I mean ghosts."

"Ghosts. What do you mean ghosts?"

"Terrifying, horrifying, wicked."

"Wicked. What do you mean?"

"Bloody hell, is that the only thing you can say?"

"What do you mean?"

"Tut!"

"Shit!" The one with the folded arms unfolded them and invaded my personal space. "That house used to belong to a witch that was drowned by the local priest many, many hundreds of years ago."

From the sparks twinkling in their eyes it was easy to see what excited these three. Stories. I turned back to the house. It still looked enchanting and I was fascinated even more now knowing that a witch had once lived there. What was a witch? Someone with magic in her heart. Someone who heard the whispers wherever she went.

Oh goody, a witch!

—TWO—

I began to learn a lot about the haunted house and my new friends. The one that did most of the talking was Suki. She had long blonde hair that was so fine and thin; one day I would discover how thin it actually was. The other girls' names were Katie and Carly. Carly looked the youngest because she was so small, but she wasn't, we were all the same age. My alleged friends all liked pink and all had blonde hair. I was the odd one out with my short black hair that my mother cut.

Since our first meeting the rest of the holidays were spent listening to the Pink Brigade and their tales concerning the haunted house. According to folk legend the house was actually the first house you came to when entering the town. In old times, the first house you came to in a village was owned by a witch. Suki and Katie seemed to do all the talking while Carly and I just sat on the kerb listening to the stories. Suki was the authority on the haunted house. One afternoon, while paying attention to what Suki was concocting about the house, I pondered a vital element.

"What was the priest's proof?"

Suki looked up. Katie puckered her lips and frowned. Carly put her head in her hands. I ventured again, "What did the priest give as evidence?"

This time though Suki had the answer.

"Rain."

"Rain?"

"Yeah, rain."

I looked on while Carly nodded her head and Katie leaned closer to listen.

"Yeah. Because it had rained for months on end. The priest claimed it was the old lady's fault."

"Well, was it winter?" Suki didn't answer, just looked at me as if I'd said leprechauns are real. I changed my way of questioning. "How did he know that?"

"Well, the priest said she'd been doing the old rope trick. See, you tie nine knots in a piece of string and as you do you name each knot. For example, mist, drizzle, rain... and when you come to the last knot you name it cloudburst."

"When did the priest say all this, then?"

Suki sniffed and raised her head in the air as she said, "The priest told his parishioners in church one Sunday morning."

"Well, it appears the priest knew more about spells and witches than the old lady." Suki and Katie peered at me. "Well, it's true," I protested.

Suki was the worst out of all of us. She played on our innocence and rallied our curiosity so it was inevitable that in the end we would have to explore the house. Katie on the other hand was more sensible and told Suki that if she wanted to get herself killed then that was fine by her, it was just that Suki was not to get us killed as well because if that happened, Katie said, her father would sue Suki for murder. Nevertheless, Suki didn't take any notice of this and clearly was not scared about going to jail for the murder of her three friends since after all she would be dead as well.

"Perhaps we should try the nine knot trick instead," Katie suggested, as she could see Carly was afraid at the prospect of going into the house.

"We don't have any string," Suki replied.

"Well, we could get some." Katie was unrelenting.

"No, I think it would be better if we just explored the haunted house, and perhaps we'll find the original piece of string."

"What, from hundreds of years ago?"

"Yeah."

"There wouldn't be anything left."

"Why?" Carly whispered.

"Because it would have decayed."

"Yeah, just like the bones of the witch."

"All eaten away by maggots and worms."

"Stop it! Stop it!" Carly screamed, putting her hands up to her ears. But Suki had leaned forward and was shouting 'worms' in her ear.

"Well, what is the spell then? What's the words Suki?"

She turned to me with a look that suggested I enjoyed stopping her having fun.

"Yeah, Suki, what is the spell, then?" Katie asked once more. Carly's hands slowly came down from her ears. Suki now had something she loved most in the world - an audience.

"Well…" She thought about it and then with an imaginary piece of string she began the spell. "With each knot you tie, you name it. You say, 'Oh rain, I call you to come when I tie these knots. Number one I shall call you mist. Number two shall be drizzle, number three I call light rain, number four…'"

As we were sitting under the shade of a tree, we didn't feel the first few spots until…

"Huh? What was that?"

"What was what?"

"There it is again."

"Shhh, I'm doing the spell, Katie."

"But its rai - "

"Shhh."

But then a few more drops of rain dripped from the cloudless sky. The others screamed and jumped away from the shade of the old tree.

"We shouldn't sit here. We shouldn't be talking about such things where it all happened," whimpered Carly. I glanced around. Suki had realised what was happening and the other two were also concerned.

"Perhaps Carly's right, perhaps we should go home now."

"Yes, perhaps we should go home NOW," shouted Suki. Then there was a crackle of thunder and with that Carly had gone. A few drops of rain later and Suki followed her.

"But it's only a thunder storm."

"Yeah, but we're under a tree. And there's not a cloud in the sky."

Then suddenly the lights went out; someone had turned off the sun. And looking up I saw a huge cloud had appeared from absolutely nowhere.

"See ya."

And Katie was gone too before I could say, 'There might be a rainbow, we could see where it ends.'

By the time I got home I looked like I'd been swimming in the dock. My hair poured water and my shoes squelched with every step. I left them near my father's bag and went upstairs to change. Halfway up the stairs someone turned the lights back on. The sun had been allowed out again and as I dried my hair in the bathroom I could hear laughing and giggling coming from our back garden. I went to the window and peaked out, though the sun made my eyes hurt from the glare of water that shone everywhere.

Mother was in the garden with my father. They were holding hands and appeared to be happy in each other's company, for once. I stared at them hardly believing my eyes, so mesmerised that I nearly missed the rainbow.

I stood at the window for a long time watching my parents just walk in the garden, holding hands in the rain while a rainbow shone over the town of secrets. It was the only time in my childhood I can remember them being so happy together, the only memory I have of my parents not yelling at each other.

The haunted house had become Suki's obsession and she dragged us into her neurosis with pinching, hair-pulling and ghost stories. She got her way.

The empty house stood alone at the end of our avenue. It didn't look right there, it looked out of place. It needed somewhere dark and mysterious, preferably overlooking a cemetery. There was something about it that made everyone feel uncomfortable. It stood like a giant eyesore always staring us in the face. No matter where we looked, it would be still be there; nothing could erase it and nowhere in the world could it ever fit in.

We waited until evening for our escapade. Dusk's cloak crept silently down and spread itself over our quiet town as I ventured out towards the house. We were to meet just outside the gates. I was there first as I didn't want to disappoint my new-found friends; I think exploring the haunted house was some kind of initiation for me. As I stood under its watchful gaze, everything fell silent. The town was still. In the dusk, the house seemed to have a perverse atmosphere even worse than in the day. It was supposed to be empty yet to me it seemed more alive than our house, a house full of screaming children and yelling parents.

Suddenly the sound of footsteps broke the silence and out of the shadows came Katie. She was closer to me than the others and she behaved older than most of us as well. She greeted me with a nod, words unnecessary. I knew she was just as petrified as me. Then more footsteps were heard. Katie and I just stared at each other and raised our eyebrows. Suki was dressed up as Wonder Woman and Carly was dressed as Batgirl.

"What the hell are you wearing?"

"And why?" My favourite question.

"They give us special powers."

"What, being a prat?"

Suki gave Katie an icy stare and insisted that their costumes gave them superhuman strength.

"The strength of a thousand men," added Carly.

"I wish you had the brains of a thousand men," I muttered. Katie laughed and Suki squinted at me.

Strangely, even though Suki and Carly had superhuman strength, they still wanted me to go first. (As the evening proceeded it turned out that the only powers they had were to run very fast in the opposite direction.)

I stared up at the house and gulped as I opened the gate and trod cautiously towards it. Each step brought me closer to the black door and soon we were all standing outside, glancing round at each other and wondering what we were going to do now. Then Suki boldly stepped forward and knocked on the door. We waited a short while then all of a sudden the door creaked as it pulled itself from the hinges and fell to the ground with a loud crash. We all jumped back in complete horror.

"That's enough for me," squealed Carly as she zoomed away down the garden path with her Bat Girl cape flowing behind her.

Suki, Katie and I looked at each other then took a brave step forward over the door and on into the house. Everywhere was quiet and there was not a sound to be heard except for our hearts pounding. We looked round and saw a light in the distance; it was dark and damp, yet for me the strange light held a certain kind of warmth and I felt drawn to it. I led the way. The light was coming from the living room. I felt no fear as we walked towards it. Then we stopped and gazed at the sight before us. Katie's and Suki's eyes were as big as saucers and both of them stood frozen like icicles, while I on the other hand was simply transfixed. I felt neither brave nor afraid at that moment, just curious.

There was a fire burning and huddled over it was an old lady, though we couldn't see her face as she was wearing a cloak with a hood which hid her features. She was stooped over and looked as if she walked with a limp. Then the old lady suddenly leaped forward towards us with a growl, startling even me. Katie and Suki quickly defrosted and ran screaming out of the house, never to return, while I tripped over and fell on the floor unable to move. The blood was pulsating round my body. I could hardly speak but the words 'Jesus, Mary and Joseph' came trembling from my lips.

The old lady came towards me; she was stooped over but not because old age had riddled her bones. It was because she was laughing so much. Her laughter took away my moment of fear. She held out her hand to pull me up and I was amazed to see that it looked so young and small. As my eyes widened she pulled the hood down so I could see her face more clearly. It was Megan. She was still laughing and I joined in. We left the house holding hands and walked home together. We probably talked but there was no conversation as such. The only word I said was "Yes" to Megan's constant "Good, huh?"

I turned round to look back at the house so I could see where our friendship had begun. But I'm sure I saw something move. The curtain in the top window seemed to fall back as if someone had been watching us the whole time. But I didn't say anything about it and neither did Megan for that matter.

—THREE—

Since our second meeting during the haunted house escapade, I found out that Megan was two years older than me though when talking with her I sounded older. Megan gave me a wonderful feeling when I was around her and I no longer felt lonely. We understood each other as we wanted to play the same games and we had no need to explore haunted houses. As for Katie and Suki, they'd also had enough of haunted houses so for the rest of the holidays they spent their time going shopping with their mothers while I played with Megan.

I was seven years old that summer and somehow the days seemed longer. Birthdays and Christmas took so long to come around and I thought the summer holidays would never end. Little did I know how precious holidays were and how priceless were the moments spent with Megan. Her silence taught me so much that I cannot put down in words. They could never say as much as the silence did.

In a short time we had become inseparable and the games we played were ones involving dressing and nursing our dolls in Megan's back yard. We made tents and played house. I found out a lot about Megan and inevitably our limited conversations turned to school. We were both starting a new school as Megan had been asked to leave the school I was going to. It wasn't that Megan couldn't do the work; it was because her mother would stand at the gates watching out for her. Apparently, some of the other parents didn't like this.

The only place where I found solace was with Megan. The innocence of her being put me at ease with myself. I no longer had to justify my actions. I just did what I wanted to do. With Megan I no longer anticipated negative words falling from her lips condemning someone whom she was jealous of, or simply did not understand. Such negative thoughts and feelings could never touch Megan. It was as if she were protected by the purity of her condition, encased in armour which acted as a shield against the corrupt negativity that surrounded us all.

In her silence, when we played with our dolls, I learned many things. I took notice of how Megan would treat empty words. She didn't even bat an eyelid when girls called her names. Her complete unawareness of the whole matter showed me how trivial it was to worry about what other people thought. I would remember this many times in the years that followed. I would need it.

Megan's mother helped bring out her toys to play in the garden. She suggested dolls' tea parties, with which we agreed and she obliged. She made cakes and little sandwiches that our dolls never ate but we did. On other days she invited me to stay and have tea with them. I accepted and often. In fact, I think I ate more times at Megan's house than my own.

Megan's mother always cooked us what we liked and as children we liked the least healthy of meals. Chips, sausages and beans were our favourite. Beans, chips and corned beef came a close second followed by eggs, beans and chips. They say variety is the spice of life. However, we would never eat the complete egg each. Megan preferred the yellow yoke and I preferred the white bit so we swapped plates and finished each other's eggs. Her mother never said anything, instead just laughed as she cleared the empty plates away and prepared the table for dessert. She always made a cake. Our favourite was chocolate sponge cake with chocolate cream oozing out of its sides. After we had finished devouring it, Megan's mother would swoop down with a wet towel and clean our faces and hands. She opened up a whole new world for me, an unhealthy food world maybe but she knew what children liked and she listened.

One day she asked me if I would like a creamy bar cola. I looked at Megan who just nodded 'Yes'. I had never had anything like this before. A huge glass of cola with a big dollop of vanilla ice cream topped off with a chocolate bar was placed in my hands with the words, "There you are, Becky, I hope enjoy it." I gazed at Megan who was too busy tucking into her creamy bar cola. I looked up at Megan's mother and smiled 'Thank you'. At last, someone who understood children; I had found an adult I could respect. Thus was my time with Megan and her mother. However, time swept by so quickly that school arrived suddenly, too suddenly.

The summer holidays were drawing to a close and I would be going to school on my own. Even though she couldn't, I still wanted Megan to come with me to my school. I could never understand why she was not allowed to. Her mother could have been told to stay away from the gates until the end of the school day. Megan was just the same as everyone else to me. Schools were for children and Megan would always be a child.

I'd never been to school in Ireland. Other children went to the local village school which Aunt Siobvon was the governor of. Aunt Siobvon was one of those family members who relished having ancestors that could be traced all the way back to the time when Ireland 'belonged to the free'. At any given opportunity she would stand up and tell of our proud heritage, of how marvellous we were as kings of our province. Thus my education was based on nationalism and history was the major subject.

Aunt Siobvon taught Leah, Peter and me for a reason. She wanted us to be top of the class. We had a right, she said, because of our heritage never to be average or normal. We had to be above average. There was never to be a dunce in the Doen family. By the time I was five, Peter and Leah were at school so it was just me that Aunt Siobvon would, for want for a better word, teach. Two hours every evening, all weekends and all school holidays were spent reading, writing, adding, subtracting, multiplying and dividing. When I got it wrong I was hit by a ruler - I learned fast.

My father never said a word against Aunt Siobvon. He couldn't tolerate a word she said and would often walk out of the room the minute she stood up for her speech on our noble family. My father never had any power over Aunt Siobvon. Come to think of it, my father never had any power over any woman.

So for most of my early life it was Aunt Siobvon who was the most domineering figure. Just like father who was away at sea, mother didn't seem to be around much; I never knew where she disappeared to, yet rumours abounded and one in particular would later completely change our world.

By the time I was seven we had finally left for England and now I was starting school for real. Mother was never really that organised, so I got my school uniform the day before term started. My father came back from one of his fishing trips and took me shopping. There was a shop in town that specialised in uniforms of all types. I had no idea where we were going but anywhere with my father seemed basically alright with me, though my heart missed a beat when we strolled into Mr Robinson's straight-jackets-for-all shop. This was cruelty. I had to wear a school tie, the most disgustingly coloured tie ever imaginable consisting of shades too lurid to write down on paper; but the horrible tie did not even match the horrible uniform, a skirt and cardigan in a repulsive brown colour.

On seeing myself in it in the mirror, I saw a reflection behind me of a beautiful pale blue uniform which I much preferred to my prison uniform.

"Why can't I have one of those uniforms? I like that colour much better than this."

"Because, Rebekah, that's not a school uniform. It's a Girl Guides' uniform." Mr Robinson explained.

"Well, okay then, I'll join the Girl Guides instead of school."

The adults looked on and ignored me.

I walked out of Mr Robinson's shop a little heavier; my father walked out with pockets a little lighter. We strolled silently down the streets. My eyes wandered upwards from the grey pavement to the red brick, to the cream curtains hanging at the eyes of houses with red roofs. Behind the rows and rows of houses soared colossal mountains made out of clouds. The soft clouds took on solid shapes that were rocky and steep. White feathery clouds mingled with grey rain nebulae giving the mountains sharp rugged corners, while the white vapour counteracted the jagged grey with soft white edges. My father noticed my silence.

"What's the matter, Rebekah?"

"The clouds look like mountains."

My father looked up. "They're just clouds, Rebekah."

"I wanna climb to the top of that cloud mountain and slide down the slippery side."

My father appeared uneasy. "You know, Rebekah, when you go to school you'll have to stop daydreaming."

"What do you mean?"

"Well, I see you at times just sitting staring into space. Like now, you were dreaming about the clouds."

"And that's daydreaming?"

"Yes. School's too important to waste the time you spend there. You're not allowed to waste the time by dreaming in school."

"But isn't school the place where dreams are made?"

He never answered. But now that my father had brought up the subject of school I wanted to continue.

"Anyway, Great-Grandpa didn't exactly have a brilliant education yet he did alright for himself and his family."

"Yes, but it was different then."

"Yeah, but he chose the one thing he knew he could do well, which was fishing, and look what happened."

"But, Rebekah, it wasn't that easy."

"Well, everyone in the family is doing alright."

"You don't know everything about the family, Rebekah. There are things about the family you wouldn't understand."

That was definitely the end of the conversation, nothing else was said. My father closed up, ever protective of some secret within our family I had no idea of. A secret that would save my life but steal my childhood.

I thought for the sake of my father that I would give school a chance; perhaps it would be better than I had imagined... Still, when Monday morning came and my father tried to wake me up, I pretended to be fast asleep; but he knew, as parents always do. I moaned and groaned as I got out of bed for the first day and came downstairs heavily and slowly. My feet felt like they were made of lead and they made a heavy thump with every step, thump, thump, thump. At last I came to the breakfast table and looked at the plate of toast my father had made me. I pushed it away. Was I upset or too excited?

"Rebekah, you must have something to eat before you go to school or you'll faint and be sent home."

I looked up at my father as a huge smile spread over my face.

"Now, Rebekah, I'm surprised at you."

I slouched back down again.

"Here, have some tea with sugar in it. That'll keep you going until you have your milk at school."

"We have milk at school?"

"Yes."

"Why?"

"Because the grown-ups want you to be strong and healthy, that's why. Now drink your tea, Becky, and then I'll take you to school."

I picked up the big mug of tea and wrapped my hands right round it so my fingers could be warmed. I watched the clock, symbolising my freedom sneaking away from me. With every passing minute I felt the prison of school slowly close its bars behind me; when I finally got out my childhood would be gone, wasted away on learning useless information. Megan would learn more at her school.

"I want to go to school with Megan."

"Megan?"

"Yes."

"Oh, Ruth Doherty's daughter?"

"Yes. I want to go to school with her."

"Well, you can't."

"Why?"

"Because Megan goes to a special school."

"So?"

"So people like you don't go there."

"Well, I'm special aren't I?"

My father smiled. "Yes, you are. But you're still not allowed to go."

"Why?"

"Because she's different, Becky. She's not like you and me. We decided she shouldn't be at the school anymore."

"We?"

"Yes, well, I'm a school governor. So hurry up, you don't want to be late!"

I didn't say a word. I knew it was no use trying to continue the conversation and just then Peter and Leah came downstairs. They behaved cordially to me but that was because my father watched every moved they made. Leah even went so far as to give me a compliment, which I think must have nearly broken her jaw.

"Oh Becky, how... how... sweet you look." She glanced at my father and gave a full teeth smile. He just raised his eyebrows in reply. As for Peter, he didn't say good morning to anyone, even my father, who just stared at him in disgust.

"Becky, have you finished your tea?"

I nodded even though there were twenty minutes at least left in the mug. I understood my father so reluctantly got up from the chair and went to get my satchel, waiting at the door for my father who had gone upstairs to tell mother that I was going. He came downstairs and sighed, opened the door and out we ventured.

Megan had not yet started on her journey to school. She was sitting on her wall at the corner of the avenue, waiting. I smiled as we walked nearer.

"Have a... n... n... nice day a... at SCHOOOOOL, Becky."

"Thank you, Megan, you too." Megan was better than a brother or sister or even a mother. She was a friend.

As we walked past the haunted house, my father seemed to quicken his pace. The leaves from trees that dominated the garden had fallen and were crushed beneath my feet. The lifeless, fading days of autumn had drifted into our world bringing the death of summer dreams and the arrival of school nightmares. The harsh days of a cold winter were dragging near, and the summer seemed so far away. There was a lot to happen before another summer. I was more unbelievably quiet than usual and my father noticed, as he usually noticed different mood swings. His extra-sensory perception was working overtime.

"You know, Rebekah, once you get to school you won't feel half as bad. It's just the getting there that makes you feel horrible."

I nodded without saying a word and we strolled on until finally we reached the gates of Hell.

The playground was full of screaming children, all hyped-up and raring to go for another year. I just felt physically sick. My stomach had so many butterflies jumping out of their cocoons that I began to think if I opened my mouth they would all fly out in a mad frenzy. My father and I walked straight into the school as 'some administrative jobs' needed to be seen to. While he sorted them out I was shown my classroom.

Miss Pike was my teacher. She was a tall, thin woman whose face was long and drawn. Her hair was tied tightly back in a bun. When Miss Pike went to fetch the other children my father came to say 'Goodbye' but I could not control my tears and they suddenly poured from my eyes as I grabbed hold of him.

"Don't leave me."

"Rebekah, Rebekah…"

"I want to go back home with you."

"Rebekah, you can't. You know you have to go to school. You can't get out of it here like you did in Ireland." He saw that this was doing no good so he tried a different angle. "Look, Rebekah, you like reading and writing, don't you?"

I nodded my head which was pressed close to my father's belly.

"Well, you'll learn to read and write that much better if you go to school and do your best."

I released my grip, swallowed some more tears and formed a smile for my father as I didn't want him to worry. "I'm sorry."

"That's okay. Now dry your tears, we don't want our new friends thinking you're a baby, do we?"

I nodded an answer and was about to ask him why he didn't want people to see me cry when children began to swarm in. My father heard them and stepped back from me.

"Well, see you tonight, Rebekah. Have a good day at school."

—FOUR—

As I watched my father walk away, I felt my lip quiver; then all of a sudden a firm voice was heard.

"Now then, Miss Doen, we will have none of that nonsense here."

I gulped the tears back and felt a firm hand place itself on my shoulder.

"Come along, Miss Doen."

The hand tightened its grip and led me to the front of the class. Miss Pike stood behind me with both hands on my shoulders. This was a nightmare. I quickly glanced around to see twenty-seven faces peering at me. Never in my life had I had so many people's attention.

"Now children, this is Rebekah Doen," Miss Pike proclaimed to the class, as I looked round for some familiar faces. Suki, Katie and Carly peered back at me. "Rebekah, we are all in groups of three except for this group here."

Miss Pike pointed to the first row of the class where three mischievous faces were staring up. At the end of the row there was one empty desk. I presumed it was mine and I was right.

"Rebekah, you will be in the Black Group so you will be a group of four. This is your desk right here." Miss Pike led me to the desk and tapped it with her finger. It was opposite Miss Pike's and she must have guessed what I was thinking. "Yes, Rebekah, your team is the worst team in the entire class, which is why it is at the front. And that it why, my dear girl, you will be sitting right next to me, so I can keep a close watch on the antics you're bound to engage in."

I sat in the chair and looked to the right to see my team mates staring at me. There were two boys, one really tall boy who towered over the others and a really small boy with hair a similar colour to Megan's, and a girl.

Our orders were to write what we had 'accomplished' in the summer holidays. However, my coming from Ireland seemed to confuse Miss Pike who had to ask, while handing out our exercise books, "Can you write, Miss Doen?"

I nodded 'Yes' but, to my surprise, instead of hearing a compliment I was answered by a harsh, "Only donkeys nod, Miss Doen." I swallowed the tears deep down into my stomach, sick at the thought that I would be here for the next ten years.

The classroom went silent. Miss Pike had given us our orders and we complied. The tall boy sighed and rubbed his head while the other one seemed enthralled by the ceiling. The boys were finding the task a wee bit difficult but the girl and I scribbled away. She looked at my page and a half of summer achievements and then at Miss Pike, whose head was down with her eyes screwed up tight as she counted out exercise books. The girl turned to me and whispered:

"Do you really have an interesting family, or is that all bullshit?"

The tall boy sniggered and Miss Pike glared at us, but continued with her counting. I acknowledged the girl. "Bullshit."

Everyone at the Black Table sniggered, drawing the attention not only of Miss Pike but also of the Pink Team who looked over to see what we were up to. Feeling her control slipping away, Miss Pike enquired if anyone at the Pink Table had finished.

"No, Miss Pike."

"Well Katie, I suggest you ignore the Black Group if you want to finish."

"Yes, Miss Pike. Sorry, Miss Pike."

"Apology accepted, Katie."

The girl beside me screwed up her face and softly mimicked, "Sorry, Miss Pike."

This time both the boys and I sniggered. Miss Pike caught me smiling.

"Miss Doen, I can see that I have placed you in the right group. But instead of having a calming effect on them, you are indeed fanning the flames of deceit and trouble that is so typical of you Irish."

I looked up and straight through her. My co-conspirators looked on, as did the rest of the class. Miss Pike, feeling the stare of twenty-seven pairs of eyes, stood up.

"I suggest the rest of you get on with the task set. This conversation concerns no-one else except Miss Doen and myself."

Everyone's head went down and there was a shuffling of papers and the sound of anxious scratching of pencils on writing books. Miss Pike turned her glare on me.

"Now, Miss Doen, I assumed with your family's good name that you would have a responsible disposition. However, it is now apparent that you have those Irish characteristics that are so damaging to the welfare of good English society."

"But, Miss Pike, she's in the Black Team."

A smile spread across our faces as Miss Pike turned to Suki.

"Explain yourself, Suki."

"Well, Miss, if you had intended Rebekah to be influenced by good English society then you should have put her in the best group, which is us. Not the Black Team which is... em... not very good people."

"Thank you, Suki, brilliantly deduced but with one flaw. I did not want Miss Doen with the Pink Team as I was concerned she may just influence you in the wrong way. I foolishly thought she would have no effect on the Black Team because they are not the best representatives of English society."

"No, but there's more of us," quickly whispered the small boy.

Miss Pike slammed her hand down onto the desk. "That will be enough from you. I do not want to hear one more sound out of you for the rest of the day, and that does include you, Miss Doen. Do you understand?"

"Yes, Miss Pike," we all mumbled.

"Is that understood, Miss Doen? Is it?"

"Yes, Miss Pike." The words fell coldly from my lips but I could sense the worry in Miss Pike's voice.

We all picked up our pencils and began to write once more. Miss Pike, sensing the insolence had passed, sat back down at her desk, picked up her red pen and began to write names on the exercise books. All was quiet and conscientious but the girl near me was really curious now.

"Where do you live, Rebekah?" she whispered, while the boys briefly glanced up and then went back to writing, well, storytelling.

Miss Pike didn't make a move. The black table was so close to her that she must have heard us but this time she merely ignored us, which was best all round. I couldn't remember the name of the street where I lived so I just replied, "Not far from school."

"Oh, do you live near the haunted house, Rebekah Doen?" she whispered softly to me, nodding her head. I stared at her with foolish innocence and wondered what she was talking about, seeing a flicker of knowing in her eyes. I was just about to ask her what she meant when all of a sudden the school bell rang. It was Break. The children in class became edgy but dared not move. Miss Pike had yet to say so. She looked up from her desk as the classroom now began to fill with the noise from the growing playground of excited children outside.

"All right class, how many people have finished?"

No hands went up. She looked at me and said, "How many people have nearly finished?"

Everyone's hand went up including mine, but her eyes had not left me.

"Miss Doen, are you sure you've nearly finished, or have you mastered the art of lying as well?"

"No, Miss Pike, I really have finished." I bit my lip at what I really wanted to say but Miss Pike must have sensed what went through my mind.

"Well, you can all put your pencils down and go to Break. You can finish your reports when you come back." There was a sound of pencils being placed on tables and the moving of chairs. The Black Team got up but Miss Pike had not yet finished. "And where do you four think you are going?"

"Out to play Miss Pike."

"And who told you to?"

We looked at one another. "You did, Miss Pike," a chorus of voices said.

"No, I did not. I told the class, not you four."

"But…"

"No buts, thank you very much, impertinent child. You can all stay in and finish your report on what you did this summer. You have Miss Doen to thank for your absence from Break."

The tall boy looked down to me and gave an 'it's okay' smile.

"I hope this punishment will make you three think twice about allowing yourselves to be influenced by an Irish idiot."

The girl grabbed my hand and I immediately released my fist. We sat down once more, picked up our pencils and began to write. Miss Pike, feeling she had the upper hand, went out and left us alone in the classroom.

"Bitch," said the girl. "Not you, Rebekah, that cow that's just gone out. She's always had it in for us."

Just then the Headmaster, Mr Lukas, came in.

"Well, well. Miss Pike tells me you've all had an eventful morning?"

We all just looked on and didn't say a word.

"Well, well. I do hope you said sorry to Miss Pike?"

That bitch will never hear those words from this mouth, said my brain.

"Well, well, carry on then, group. I hope I don't have to speak to you again."

He went out as he'd come in - tense, worried and completely lacking in any respect.

"Well, well," mimicked the tall boy. "We'd better finish this."

"Well, well, yes indeed," I replied.

The girl turned to me. "You're gonna fit right in here, Rebekah Doen. Miss Pike did place you in the right group. And no, you're not gonna have a bad influence on us, but we'll have a bad influence on you."

Miss Pike walked back in with a hot cup of coffee. "I see I can't even trust you for a minute." We didn't reply nor look up at her. As she sat down at her desk she mumbled, "I even have to give up my Break just to keep an eye on you."

We continued our work and never uttered another word, trying not to laugh as my group pulled faces at one another. When the dinner bell finally rang, Miss Pike said we could go and we all scrambled out of the classroom to the playground. The day was warm yet the sun did not have the same glow, just a hazy orange colour. I stepped out into it and was soothed.

The whole morning had been rather eventful to say the least. I had done what I was told yet Miss Pike had still made me feel like a bad child. I went to the very far corner of the playground, refusing to let myself cry, and didn't see the girls come and huddle round me.

"Why don't you come and play with us, Becky?"

I peered up to see Katie and co. They were curious about the morning's events. I looked at the three of them but knew I could not last long with them.

"Boy, Miss Pike sure doesn't like you!" said Carly.

I was amazed at this as Carly was the quiet one of the group who never said anything except in times of debate when she was either on Katie's side or Suki's. I always stayed in the corner with my own thoughts.

"Really? What, you really think Miss Pike was picking on me?"

"Yes."

"Oh good. I thought I was the only one with that idea."

"No, everyone thought it."

And everyone had kept quiet, I thought, as I felt the anger welling up inside me.

"Fancy putting you in the Black Team with those three." Katie pointed to my three dubious looking team mates who were slouched against the playground wall staring at me with the same curiosity as I had towards them. I turned to Katie.

"Why? What's wrong with them? Are they really terrible?" I was worried that my team mates might just be hoodlums but thankfully I was not to be disappointed. They were hoodlums and I would have a great time.

"No, not terrible, more stupid than anything. They can't do their work so then they get bored and start distracting everyone and - "

Suki interrupted. "Becky, don't worry, they're only stupid and you know all about dunces as you spent your summer holidays with spasmo Megan."

Once again my hand fell into a fist. But then I thought of how Megan would have reacted to Suki's comment so I ignored it and stormed away. I marched across the playground to my team mates and thought about the colour black. I realised that it was the most colourful of colours as all the colours of the spectrum flowed through it like a rainbow. They glanced round at each other when they realised I was coming over to them. This was the first time we had had the opportunity really to talk and get to know one another. Megan was constantly in my thoughts and I felt brave.

"Hello."

"Hi… ummm," they simultaneously mumbled. I looked round quickly at my team mates, at the wall they leaned on, the ground they stood on, back again to their faces. Megan.

"Well, you all know my name."

The girl lifted her head up and glanced at the boys who were gazing at the grey pavement of the playground. She looked at me. "Yeah, my name's Liza."

"Oh, hi Liza." I looked expectantly to the boys.

"I'm Nigel and this Billy."

"Hi. You're really tall, Nigel. How old are you?"

"Seven."

"Oh." So much for me trying to make conversation. Though we had no Miss Pike breathing down our necks, we still didn't say a word to each other again until the bell rang for us to go in for dinner.

"Come on," said Liza, running to join the line. Billy ran past me knocking me aside, not knowing his own strength.

"Come on. It's time for dinner." Nigel placed his hand on my shoulder and we joined the ever-growing line.

"What the hell are we doing?"

"We have to march like this, left, right, left, right." Nigel marched into school with the rest of the boys' line.

"Why do we have to march?"

"Don't know, we just do," Billy whispered as he marched past.

"Shush!"

"What?"

"We're not allowed to talk."

"Jesus! This is worse than being in Miss Pike's class."

My team mates all had packed lunches and as they sat at the same table as me, eating sandwiches and discussing what type of chocolate they had, I was soon to find out why. We were all paralysed by a painful scream. It was Suki. She stood up and I could see the tears streaming down her face. One of the dinner ladies came rushing up to ask her what the matter was; apparently Suki had lost one of her teeth biting into the mashed potatoes.

I stared at Liza in utter disbelief and she just looked back at me and raised her eyebrows. "See, we're not as dumb as everybody thinks we are." And she took a huge bite out of her sandwich. From that day on I never had a school dinner and always took a packed lunch.

In the weeks that followed I looked forward to seeing my team mates. They were to become my wildest friends, with whom I would have the most fun. We were to be partners in crime, comrades in dangerous times. Yet secrets and lies were also to rise up like a wave crashing over me.

—FIVE—

I went home happy that day. I walked with Liza as she lived round the corner from me. I had found that out in the afternoon Maths lesson. Apparently Liza could only communicate with a threat of detention over her. The sun shone down in the half-past three sky, the clouds drifting like white candy floss that had been stretched and stretched until there were just minute wisps. Sickly sweet clouds scattered here and there in a bowl full of the deepest blueberry syrup.

My mind was full of thoughts about my father. He had not come to collect me from school on my very first day. I wondered what his excuse would be this time. Contemplating this, it was hardly surprising that I had forgotten exactly where I was.

"Where are we?"

"Don't you know?"

Liza stopped walking. Her hand was placed most expertly on her hip. Suddenly I could imagine her leaning in the doorway of a terraced house, wearing an apron and chattering to the next door neighbour while her children played in the street. I looked at her as if I'd been scolded.

"I haven't been here that long," I pleaded.

It worked. Liza's hand released its dominating pose on her hip and she commenced walking once more. I continued my plea of innocence.

"Even in Ireland, you know, I used to forget where I was."

"You're kidding?"

"No. I even used to forget how to get home from the village shop."

"What did your parents say?"

"Well, mother told me off. Peter and Leah called me stupid. But my Daddy told me to get my bearings right."

"Your what?"

"My bearings. He showed me in our garden back in Galway where east was and where west was."

"Well, did you learn anything?"

"No. But I enjoyed it all the same."

"Why?"

"I was with my Daddy."

That's all that was said, all that was needed. Liza was silent and we didn't say anything else until we reached the haunted house, which I was to find Liza was the authority on.

"It's 'aunted, you know."

"Is it really, now?"

Liza had no idea of my escapade there or that Megan was the ghost.

"Yeah! They say it's 'aunted by the spirit of a mad woman."

"A mad woman! I thought - "

"A witch?"

"Yeah."

"Oh no, that story's wrong. I'm right."

"Oh. How do you know?"

"Because I've seen lights in that house at night."

The knitting of my eyebrows must have betrayed my confusion.

"My house is actually at the back of yours. But my bedroom faces this house so I can look out of my window and see what's going on there." I followed her pointed finger to a bedroom window that had so many teddy bears staring out of it I was surprised she could see anything at all out of her window.

"You've got a lot of teddy bears."

"Thanks. Wanna see my bedroom? "

"Some other time, eh? I have to get home. My parents might be worried." What a joke, but I thought it sounded good.

"Sure. Listen, anytime you wanna see my room just pop round when you feel like it."

"To be sure."

"Well, see ya tomorrow, Becky."

"Aye, see ya tomorrow."

Liza walked on home and I turned the corner to walk down the avenue when suddenly I heard the thumping of heavy feet on the pavement. I looked up just as I was nearly knocked down by my arrogant brother.

"Hey squirt, get out the bloody way."

"This pavement's not just yours, Peter."

"Up yours, Daddy's girl. Oh, by the way, Pa's gone back on a fishing trip."

My heart sank into my stomach dragging my mouth down with it. "Wh… what do you mean? He never told me he was going."

"Well, little one, you never can tell with Pa."

"You're full of shit, Peter. Anyway, how do you know?"

Peter's eyes were screwed up so tightly they looked like two slits of contempt. Right at that moment I would have liked to knock him to the ground. Sadly however, there's extrasensory perception in our family so Peter turned his head away and avoided direct eye contact with me.

"Well, at school I met Tony Quinn whose father sails with Pa, you know, and he was talking about his Pa getting ready for a trip this evening."

"How do you know Daddy's going?"

"Tony said that Pa was round at his house talking about the trip."
"When does she sail?"
"Tide time."
"And what time by the hour is tide time?"
"I think its round half-four this week, little one."

I grabbed hold of his wrist and looked at his watch; it was twenty to four so maybe I still had time. I turned round and ran, completely oblivious to what Peter was shouting behind me. It had been an instantaneous decision. I just had to see my Daddy. I had no idea why. Something else was taking me. I was no longer in control of my own actions.

I ran along the streets, frantic, as if behind me stalked a huge monster wanting to catch and devour me. I didn't want to face whatever was chasing me, whatever I was frightened of. Somehow I knew my way as I ran through the streets to the docks, though I had never been to this part of town before. Moments ago I didn't even know where I lived, yet I felt I knew the way and would know my way home later. As I neared my journey's end I was running silently through the streets. Not a sound could be heard except inside, the sound of my own heart pounding furiously in my chest. My head throbbed as if to burst with madness and fury, my mind and body conspiring against me.

Suddenly I stopped running and began to walk down towards the harbour. Then and only then did calmness come over me, though like a stranger. The air felt different, cooler than the air in town, and the smell of the sea was carried along by the wind. I licked my lips, tasting the salt. The bracing clean air sparkled and tingled upon the skin.

I searched the harbour and saw my Daddy boarding a ship with Tony Quinn's father. I ran down to them yelling, "Daddy, Daddy." My father saw me and jumped back onto the quay as I ran into his arms and snuggled my face into his stomach.

"Rebekah, what the hell have you come all this way for?"

"You didn't ask me how school was. And you didn't come to get me. And you didn't tell me you were going on a trip. And how long will you be gone this time?" I waited for an answer but I knew he had none. And I never wanted to hear the truth - truth was a secret that my father never told me and I had to find out the hard way.

"Rebekah, how would you like to come fishing with me when you break up for half-term?"

I mumbled 'Yes' but deep down I knew that seeing was believing.

"Becky, darling, I have to go."

"Why?"

"Tide time's wasting."

"No, why do you have to go?"

"I just have to."

"Why can't you just stay for a month?"

"I have to work."

I released my grip. "Did you argue with mother?"

"Now, don't go upsetting yourself about your mother."

"What has she done now?"

"Becky, darling, I have to go." My father put me to one side and got back onto the boat. "Come on, Tony, let's get out of here." The ship slowly began to chug away from the dock. "Remember, I'll take you fishing when I get back, darling."

I nodded but knew it was useless to depend on any of his promises. I waved goodbye to my father as his ship plodded out of the dock gates, then I turned round and walked slowly home.

The breeze that had been so invigorating before now whistled and penetrated deep into me. I crossed my arms as I walked the grey pavements towards our house, my head permanently down, my chin nearly resting on my chest as I hugged myself tighter. A few people hurried past on their way home from work but I never saw anyone. I didn't see faces, only feet.

Then as I looked up to cross a road I saw it. I saw its tall trees come into view and knew I was nearly home. Its tall roof pointed to the heavens and as I turned the corner I saw its eyes peering at me. The paint had cracked on the window frames and parts had fallen away. The grey nets did not detract from the eyes' dismal stare. My pace slowed even more until I was almost standing still, staring at this sad, beautiful house. I tried to imagine it the way it must have been when a family lived in it, alive with light and warmth, laughter pervading every room from a family in blissful happiness.

I turned towards my own house... a family! Mother yelled at me. Peter teased me and Leah pulled my hair. Nothing was mentioned about my first day at school. No questions were asked about whether I had enjoyed or hated it. While I had tea, I compared school to home and decided there was no comparison; in fact school was better, even if it did have Miss Pike. Tea consisted of dried-up beans on soggy toast and mother exclaimed she was not going to make my tea again; it was my own fault I had not come home when it was ready. She said I had two choices, either to eat it or leave it. I ate what I could and went upstairs to my bedroom.

My room was at the far end of the house, small and compact but it housed just me and a couple of spiders. I certainly didn't mind sharing my bedroom with spiders; if they didn't bother me then I wouldn't bother them. So in nearly every ceiling corner of my bedroom there hung a spider's web. I did not have as many toys and teddy bears as I imagined Liza had, though I had a few dolls that Aunt Siobvon had given me over the years. These were dolls with porcelain faces, arms and legs, lavishly dressed in the finest of clothes. Thus I found it relatively impossible to play with them as I had to be extra careful, even though they were mine to play with; I dreaded the thought of breaking one for fear of mother.

I lay on my bed thinking of school and the Black Team. Liza would be a better friend than any of the Pink Team and the boys were completely wild. Every lesson would be a game of fun. They didn't really disrupt the lessons as no-one bothered with them.

Miss Pike's attitude towards me did not improve and her natural distaste for children as a whole never vanished. She knew instinctively how to torture a child and that mental cruelty was the best weapon when it came to discipline. Her instrument of blackmail was always Break time, those fifteen minutes of freedom we were allowed.

And every day it was the same... the bloody school milk. By mid-morning Break the milk had arrived, very warm and just about to turn. The little bottles rattled as the caretaker dumped the crate next to the door. I had not yet been introduced to the caretaker but our friendship would develop in years to come; he was Billy's uncle, which probably added to the fact that he became one of our greatest allies. Jack the caretaker dug deep into his faded blue overalls pocket to produce a cheap plastic bag of straws, which he threw onto the crate of near-curdled milk as he walked out of the door. The whole scene was conducted without a word from either Jack or Miss Pike, as she stood at the opposite end of the room watching with disgust at his audacity to come into her room without first asking permission and without even a hello or a goodbye.

Miss Pike would sigh with superiority when Jack shut the door. Then she turned to the class.

"Now, as you're probably aware the milk has arrived. I have to, by law, allow you to drink it."

The bell startled us. Children escaped from their classes, screaming into the playground, while Miss Pike stood militantly waiting, prolonging our yearning to join our comrades. After what seemed like eternity, she declared, "The girls may collect their milk one table at a time, starting with the Pink Table."

Meekly, Suki got up and went to fetch her milk, then Katie, Carly and so on. The class sat patiently drinking their milk. Every minute that ticked away was another precious moment lost in the playground. The milk was warm and an odour of crusty decay surrounded the bottles. But we had to drink it. It was good for us.

I hate milk. It tasted almost like buttermilk but with one distinction; this milk was English.

—SIX—

Father had stayed away on a fishing trip for twenty days when I thought he would only be gone for ten. When he did eventually come home he only stayed a day then went out again. One night I counted up in my head how many times I had seen my father in six weeks; it came to a grand score of three whole days. I fell asleep while trying mathematically to stretch three days into six weeks. It was better than counting sheep.

Leading up to half-term, I enjoyed school tremendously. I was right about the boys - they were wild, especially the day Nigel earned his nickname. One day we were having a Science lesson and the unlit Bunsen burner stood quietly on the wooden desk while the teacher told the class how important the Bunsen burner was in a laboratory. Billy was quick on the mark.

"How could that be the most important thing? I thought the most important thing in a Science lab was the scientist."

At this we all giggled. The teacher, having been warned about the Black Group, immediately turned to us and looked expectantly curious. We stopped giggling and he proceeded to light the Bunsen burners. I have no idea why he chose ours first; maybe he just had a death wish or maybe he wanted to see us dead. He lit the Bunsen burner and a blue flame appeared, then went on to light the other groups' burners. While he did this, Billy discovered that at the bottom of the burner was a sort of little door that opened and closed. As the teacher was telling the class what we should draw, Nigel leaned over the burner to get his pencil just as Billy opened the little door and before we could say anything Nigel's hair went WHOOSH!

Our mouths fell open at the sight. The teacher still had his back to us and we quickly tried to put out the fire in Nigel's fringe. But we couldn't stop laughing. We kept hitting Nigel on the head to put out the fire but the pressure of the situation combined with the idea of being caught only added to our hysteria. Liza and I put our heads down on the desk, explosive laughter filling our mouths but we were too frightened to let go. Billy managed to put out the fire. However, the front of Nigel's hair still smouldered.

When at last the teacher turned round, our group sat up and looked straight at him. He stared at us and knitted his eyebrows together as he squinted to get a better look. We all sat with straight backs and straight faces, though we were laughing inside. Nigel sat like us, though his hair silently smouldered away complete with bluish smoke rising from it.

Nigel's hair was not terribly damaged, just singed a wee bit, though his nickname from that day on suited him well: the Towering Inferno.

Every day after school my time would be spent with Megan and weekends were full of Megan too. Her mother began to tell me about their family as they had also originated from Ireland, the Doherty's from Derry. They were strict Catholics and Megan was taken to church by her mother nearly every evening and three times on Sundays. I thought this quite odd as we were, as Aunt Siobvon would say, of a fine noble Irish family but we had nothing to do with the church in England. I did ask my father what we were and he briskly said "Nothing." He also said sharply that religion was only there for people who were religious and we were most certainly not.

Mrs Doherty always made me smile and gave me a cuddle when I went round to play with Megan. I had to avoid meeting Suki and the gang who were rather offended that I preferred Megan to them; they would hover at the bottom of the avenue waiting for me, though I would always slip out of the back door to Megan's. Once, Leah caught me sneaking out.

"Why don't you go out the front door?"

"I don't wanna meet Katie and they lot. I don't like the things they say about Megan."

"Too much for ye? Can't stand the truth, eh?"

I slammed the back door shut and wished I was back at school. The half-term had gone so slowly and it was not until the Thursday that my father finally arrived home. I was already in bed reading when he came in to see me. Peter and Leah were downstairs with mother; I suppose the moment my father saw them all together he probably felt like he had fallen overboard into shark infested waters. He opened the door, rather sheepishly for him.

"May I come in?"

"Sure."

He sat down gently on the edge of the bed and I waited for him to begin, as I had not forgotten his promise about going on the boat.

"I'm sorry."

This is it. Here it comes.

"I'm sorry things round here are difficult."

His head went down and I looked at him, my eyes widening as I had never before heard my father speak like this. It seemed like his voice was trapped in a bottle, an SOS floating here and there, bouncing up and down through calm waters and storms, but never quite reaching the shore until it was too late to be saved.

"I know it's hard for you, Rebekah… new town, new school, making new friends. But I know you can manage it." He stopped, the message in the bottle swept away again on a passing tidal wave of pride. "How about coming on the boat with me tomorrow? You know, I did promise you."

He must have seen the look on my face. The look of total disbelief as my father had never kept a promise to me in all the years I had known him. This was really quite a long time bearing in mind I was seven.

"I have tried, Rebekah. I have tried to keep my promises but sometimes circumstances beyond my control don't allow me to carry them out. So will you come on board? "

"Of course I will."

"Now, that's grand."

I smiled back at him.

"Aye. Well, better get some sleep then, we sail quite early."

"Aye aye, Captain," I replied and flopped down into bed. He pulled the blankets up round me and ruffled my hair, said goodnight and left. That was as close as the bottle ever got to the shore.

We sailed out of the dock and round near the shore as my father said he had placed a few nets in the sea the night before. The crew was just him, Ben Hoames and me. Ben was the youngest of the usual crew but nevertheless he was at the wheel. Tony Quinn did not come, he stayed home with his wife and Tony Quinn Junior. I guess he could be called a family man.

I had the distinct feeling that this trip was really for me and my father had laid the nets especially for me. We came to where the nets had been laid and Ben and my father went to pull them in. They heaved one in and with a loud crash it bounced onto the deck. It was just a small net yet it had a good amount of wriggling fish making it look bigger than it actually was. A net full of fish, all wriggling and frantically trying to get free. They all looked the same to me with big, round frightened eyes and slippery silver bodies. However, there was one in particular that looked different to the others. It was small and it peered at me with its gormless stare as I breathed in its difference. All of a sudden my father grabbed it by the neck, looked at it and then threw it quickly back over the side. My eyes followed it as it fell back into the deep, murky waters once more. I turned expectantly to my father.

"It wasn't the same. If it doesn't look right, we don't want it."

I stood silent on the deck while my father continued to haul the fish in.

The half-term was basically over and I spent the weekend with Megan who had discovered a new sort of play. Well, it was nearly a game as everything was a game to Megan. Within her cocoon the child would never grow. My dreams, my hopes and fears were safe with Megan. I often wondered if Mrs Doherty knew how lucky she was to have a child who would remain a child forever.

Megan's new game was simply reading. I would have to read to her in the nursery. Her house was similar to ours inasmuch as it was big. But whereas in our house all the bedrooms were used, in Megan's house there was a lot of space. Her father had died when she was only two, so Megan could not remember him. The two bedrooms at the front of the house had been joined together, creating one giant room that was decorated in rainbows and clouds; this was Megan's nursery.

In fact, one could not go anywhere in the house without seeing something of Megan's. On the walls were pictures of her as a baby having her first bath and pictures of her taking her first steps. Furthermore, nearly every drawing Megan had ever done was framed and placed on a wall. Mrs Doherty claimed she had no need for other people's pictures when her daughter could draw just as well so there were no other pictures except those of Megan and the ones that she had drawn, painted or scribbled. These consisted of anything from wibbly-wobbly lines to rainbows and balloons, which I had the distinct feeling Megan had a weakness for.

After we had returned to school, I still went to see Megan in the evenings as I had a couple of hours to spare before getting ready for bed. I wanted to get out of the house anyway. Leah was having her bedroom redecorated and mother didn't want her breathing in any paint fumes at night, so Leah was put in 'the spare room', which was my bedroom. So my only sanctuary had been taken over by an older sister who had attended the Machiavellian school of play. Suffice to say, I avoided her even more than normal. My dolls were cleared away and my spiders, who must have known somehow, decided to leave of their own accord. For those few days Leah took over; make-up, hairbrushes, jewellery and magazines were strewn all over the place. I could say that my sister was a bit of a pig but I know they're extremely clean animals, so I'll just say she was a slob.

However, although I avoided her most of the time, one particular night I came to realise how human and how much like me she was.

Things had gone from bad to worse in our house. My father hardly ever came home, yet one evening very late he did. We were all upstairs curled up in our beds fast asleep, or so they thought. As if in a dream I heard the door gently close, everything around me hidden in the pitch black of night. After a while my eyes grew accustomed to the dark and I noticed a white light underneath the door. I could hear Leah breathing, turned to the wall with her covers wrapped round her and nearly over her head. The night felt so still and quiet yet the light pulled me closer to it, the curiosity too much to bear. I knew it must be my father, so I crept quietly out of bed so as not to wake Leah and walked to the door, the thin light looming bigger. I opened the door just wide enough for me to fit through. Then I was standing in it, the white light of heated words.

The stair light was on and I could hear angry voices. I knew it was my parents and I wanted to know what was being said this time. I sat on the fourth stair from the bottom and listened with a confused mind.

"Don't start with all that again, Amy. It was your bloody idea to come back."

"Only because I wanted to get away from Ireland and your damn family."

"My family, is it?"

"Aye."

"Well, that's bloody rich. Can you understand not wanting to live down the street from that?"

"You bastard. How can you say that about your own sister?"

"Don't you dare call that person my sister. I don't even know her."

"And whose fault is that?"

"Sure as hell isn't mine."

"Oh, isn't it? Well, I'm sorry, but I think it is your bloody fault. You never made one visit to see her in that institution and you never tried to get her out. You don't give a shit about her. That makes me sick. And the thought of you makes me sick."

"Well, words do no justice to describe what you make me feel."

I stood up and retraced my steps. I knew one of them would come storming out quite soon.

"Where are you going?"

"I'm going to sleep on the boat. I'll go anywhere to get away from you."

"Oh, that's right. Just fuck off, won't you? Just because you can't take the truth. You coward!"

The living room door swung open and my father stomped out, carrying his coat. Moments before his bag had just been dropped at the front door; now it was in use again. The last words I heard him mumble were "Bloody bitch." The front door slammed shut and that was the last I saw of my father for two months.

I crept back to the bedroom. I could hear mother crying as I slowly closed the door. I got into bed.

"It's best just to pull the blankets up round you."

A voice out of the darkness warmed the cold, silent bedroom of two sisters.

—SEVEN—

Secrets. Secrets in my family. Secrets you were not allowed to refer to. Secrets surrounded my childhood. Even Megan and her mother had a secret from me, though it was not to stay a secret for long.

One evening in particular I was playing with Megan up in her nursery. I was sitting on one of the huge beanbags reading about a child who never grew up and who lived in a faraway land with mermaids and pirates and lost boys. I thought Megan and I could be lost children. Mrs Doherty came in carrying some sandwiches and creamy bar cola.

"Gosh, you are lucky, Megan. You've got lots of friends now."

Megan looked up to her mother.

"I've just had a 'phone call from your old friend, she's coming round to play. She says sorry she hasn't come sooner but she's busy with school."

Mrs Doherty smiled. Her eyes seemed to expose a secret that she'd been keeping from me for a long time. After she'd gone out of the room I looked at Megan but she just smiled that huge smile of hers, her cheeks pushed so right up that her eyes nearly closed. Suddenly we heard a knock at the door. I listened tentatively. I could hear Mrs Doherty talking then the front door closed and I heard footsteps bouncing up the stairs and approaching the nursery. The door slowly opened and in bounced Liza.

My jaw hit the floor. Megan jumped up and Mrs Doherty said, "Look, Megan, your old friend Liza has come to play with you." Turning to me, she asked, "You do know Liza, don't you, Rebekah?"

I nodded.

"Well, that's alright then." And with that Mrs Doherty went out, shutting the nursery door behind her as my eyes followed her. After she'd gone I turned to Liza.

"I didn't know you knew Megan."

She nodded and smiled.

"Well, why didn't you tell me?"

"I was letting you get to know Megan better. It's true, Becky. I didn't want to interfere."

"Well, how long have you known Megan?"

"Oh yeah, we've known each other for yonks. We've been friends for ages."

And with that she went and sat down with Megan. Liza's presence here felt normal, though she didn't want to listen to any stories. She wanted to create them, so we began to play with Megan's dolls' house. The dolls' house was decorated exactly the same as her own house, including the same pictures that Megan had painted, the only difference being that they were smaller. I was intrigued.

"Who helped you to make the house?"

"Mammy!"

Nothing else was said, there was no need for explanations. The answer was clear and crisp. However, Liza grew impatient with dolls and the little house.

"You know what's needed?"

Megan looked up. I asked for her, "What?"

"Teddy bears."

We looked at each other.

"There's not a bear in sight."

"But it's a dolls' house."

"I know and that's precisely why we need some bears. Come on, Becky, come and help get some of my bears."

"Okay."

"We'll be back in a jiffy, Maggie."

"Oookay! See you lll… later all… igator!"

"In a while, crocodile."

They really did know one another well. Liza and I didn't say a word as we raced round to her house. Just as we reached the door it opened.

"Hey, bear head."

"Hey Paul, move out of the way."

Liza pushed her brother away and he just laughed. I was amazed that he didn't hit her back. I followed Liza on upstairs. I realised that I had never really talked to Liza before because in school we were busy annoying Miss Pike. I didn't know anything about her but I was to learn that she knew more about me than I did myself.

"How may brothers have you got?"

"Four."

"Four? Yuk!"

"Oh, not really, they're okay."

"You the only girl, then?"

"Yes."

"Must be lucky."

As we reached the top of the stairs Liza opened her bedroom door and a mass of teddy bears greeted me. The shelves, the windowsill and the bed were so covered with teddy bears that the floor had been taken over by them as well.

"Mother Mary o'God!" were the first words that sprang to mind.

"Got a lot, haven't I?"

"Where did you get them all?"

"Oh, from my family. Wherever my brothers or Mum and Dad go they always buy me a teddy bear."

"They must be always going somewhere," I mumbled.

"Here look, you take ten and I'll take ten."

Liza bundled my arms full of teddy bears and with that we went back to Megan's. But while walking down the street we met Katie, Suki and Carly; they stepped in our way and wouldn't let us pass.

"Going to play with Megan, are we?"

"Yeah. What's it to you, Suki? Are you going to let us pass, then?"

"Why? What are you going to do about it if we don't, Liza?"

The three of them huddled together. It appeared Suki was now the boss as Katie said nothing and just stood with her hand on her hip chewing gum. Her mouth occasionally blew a bubble which she popped then chewed some more.

"Oh grow up, Suki," Liza ordered as she pushed past, still clutching onto her teddy bears. As we walked up to Megan's house I had the distinct feeling someone was watching. I turned round expecting to see Suki and the others but I saw no-one. Instead, I looked up to the haunted house. In the window opposite Megan's nursery I could have sworn I saw a face peering out at me. I did see the net curtain fall back quickly but I didn't tell either Megan or Liza as I didn't want to frighten them. However, soon I was to find out that they knew more than me concerning the haunted house.

The curtain falling gently back became a regular occurrence, until every time I walked past the house I would stare at it until I was sure that the curtain had moved or I had seen a shadow. Liza walked with me to school but she never said anything. I always thought that she never looked at the house but perhaps I just assumed that she was not particularly bothered about the antics that had gone on there.

The Christmas Term at school was an interesting one to say the least. Miss Pike decided not to decorate the classroom. Her insect display was just as good, she declared. Miss Pike's classroom was constantly Hallowe'en, always scary. The rest of the school was sort of Christmassy and our Santa Claus was definitely Billy's Uncle Jack, the caretaker. A sort of mischievous, magical grown up who made us feel safe and showed us that adults can be fun. I don't think he ever lost his sense of wonder.

A couple of weeks before we were due to break up for Christmas, the Black Team decided to give Miss Pike a present. We were undecided as to what exactly it should be but then Billy found the perfect gift. Uncle Jack still performed his morning ritual of disturbing Miss Pike with milk and straws and one morning in particular he was even more annoying to her as he came in chewing gum. Not any ordinary gum, but space-dust gum.

The Black Team gazed longingly at each other when he came in. His mouth crackled and popped as he strode over to plonk the milk crate down near Miss Pike. She winced and leaned back slightly. Uncle Jack stood up straight, stretched his back, let out a deep sigh and began to blow a huge bubble with Miss Pike standing next to him. She coughed expectantly. The bubble crackled and popped as it grew larger and larger, nearly covering Uncle Jack's face so that only his eyes peered out over the noisy bubble. The classroom was silent at this spectacle, only the sound of the chewing gum could be heard until Miss Pike coughed again. The bubble burst. Uncle Jack swallowed the bubble gum into his mouth in one gulp, snapping his jaw shut. He then strolled over to the door where he turned back to Miss Pike and the class and said, "Merry Christmas, Miss Pike." He winked at her, saluted and left.

Miss Pike didn't move and neither did the class. The school bell startled us all, including Miss Pike who merely mumbled to us, "Come and get your milk." She sat down behind her desk as we did so and then we simply went out into the playground, as she hadn't bothered saying anything to us. She just sat in her chair, sort of staring into space. In the playground, some others called to us.

"Where did your uncle get that chewing gum, Billy?"

"Yeah, we've been trying for yonks to get some at Mr Mcenfry's shop."

"I don't know."

"Do you think he'll be able to get us some?"

Billy stared at us. You could literally see the idea going through his head. "Let's go and ask him, shall we?"

We sneaked round the corner of the playground to Uncle Jack's office. The door was open, the kettle was on and music was playing. He saw us loitering by the door. "Now then, my favourite prisoners, you've managed to escape from her clutches, eh? Well, come on in and have a seat. I don't often get visitors."

We eagerly stepped forward into Uncle Jack's domain.

"Now then, what can I do for you, Billy?"

"Hello, Uncle. Nothing much."

"Oh yeah? Just passing were you?"

"Yeah, sort of... Uncle, where did you get that chewing gum from?"

"What? Me spoggy?"

"Aye."

"It's good, in'it? Really annoyed that old she-dragon teacher of yours din'it?"

"It sure did, Uncle Jack."

We all waited anxiously for those immortal words then...

"Here, do you wanna try some? I've got plenty." Holding a full box of amazing space-dust chewing gum, Uncle Jack smiled knowingly when we seized on this wonderful invention.

"Thank you," we all murmured after we had shoved it in our mouths. After a couple of chews it started to pop with little explosions on the tongue and your teeth tingled with it.

"Here, take a couple of extra ones for later. You never know what you could do with it if you have enough," winked Uncle Jack.

We merrily crackled our way into the playground, drifting to our corner and stopping here and there to annoy the other kids with our open mouths blowing bubbles in their faces. About five minutes later the chewing gum still crackled but it tasted disgusting. Whatever flavour it had had disappeared and in return left a horrible, sticky yellow-green goo that stuck to our fingers and anything we put it on. Billy grinned at us.

"You know what? This would be a great present for Miss Pike."

"She'd never eat this."

"Yeah, she only eats dead men's fingers and tadpole soup."

"No you're missing the point, people. We don't have to get her to eat this." Billy raised his eyebrows and nodded to us. "In fact, it's going to the other end."

We peered confusedly at Billy.

"What say you, we happen to place the chewing gum on a chair, a particular chair?"

"She'd see it."

"Not if we distract her before she sits down."

"Well, what will happen?"

"Her arse will crackle."

"Billy!"

At that the bell rang and we ran, shocked, to the line. Over the next couple of days, Billy put an intricate web of plans into our heads. The event was planned for Lunch Break, giving us enough time to get in and out without being discovered by the teachers, as they usually went out for lunch.

Sneaking back into school was no problem, but escaping back out was. Further, by some twist of fate Miss Pike came back from lunch early. After we had stuck the gooey gum on the chair, Liza and I kept lookout at the door. "Come on, Billy, we've got to go."

"I just wanna make sure everything is normal."

"What for? This is Miss Pike's class. We're the Black Team. What kind of normal were you hoping for? "

"Oh no!" Liza and I exclaimed. "Miss Pike's just come round the corner."

"Shit! Oh shit!"

"Oh my God! What do we do?"

Panic ensued as we ran round the classroom searching for a place to hide.

"Shit!" exclaimed Billy again.

Miss Pike's footsteps could be heard getting closer and closer. But then we heard another footstep, a heavier one coming in the opposite direction.

"Who the hell is that?"

All four of us hid behind the door, pressed so hard into each other we thought we'd squeeze ourselves into the wall. Miss Pike was just at the door. Then suddenly the fire alarm shocked us and our breathing stopped.

"Oh Miss Pike, I wouldn't go into the classroom if I were you. That's the fire alarm."

"I know what the noise is, thank you very much. I just want to put my bag in my desk."

"I'm afraid you can't do that, Miss Pike. Fire drill. You have to go now."

"Well, really, of all the…" She tottered off down the corridor still mumbling as the door opened and we took a deep breath.

"Come on, you little horrors. Better get out of here before she comes back."

"Uncle Jack!" we breathed a sigh of relief.

"What are you up to anyway? Ah, you've done something with that spoggy ent'ya? "

"We've put it on her chair."

Uncle Jack laughed. "Oh, lovely."

There was of course no fire, it had been 'a spontaneous fire drill', claimed Uncle Jack. However, strange also that Miss Pike's chair had no chewing gum on it when we returned. We were not too disappointed, though Nigel said he would have really liked to see Miss Pike's arse crackle. Still, we knew the planned event was better in our imaginations than in reality. It probably wouldn't have worked.

Christmas. That word for me now as an adult conjures images of presents in the shops from October, money lenders urging us to 'Buy now, pay Easter', Christmas decorations alongside Hallowe'en masks. My personal response as an adult is a sigh of deep depression, a sense of unhappiness and a dread of how much I am going to have to spend this year.

As for Christmas back then, in those days of Megan and the haunted house, my personal response was a sigh of deep depression, a sense of unhappiness and a dread of how long I was going to have to spend with relatives in Ireland.

That year in particular, I simply did not want to go. Christmas brought the strangeness out in my family (though full moons had a weird effect on them as well). Every year for as long as I can remember, my parents would put on a special show of happiness and warmth in each other's company, but only at Christmas time. I called this the Christmas Miracle. However, the Christmas Miracle did not touch the rest of our family or indeed, as far as I could tell, the rest of the world.

Megan especially became a victim once more. She had been practising since Hallowe'en to be in her church choir and she really had a unique voice. She gave Liza and me a special preview. We sat on the bean bags and listened patiently while Megan sang 'Silent Night' with full zest. After she had finished we stood up and clapped, but eternity's child could not handle so much attention. She put her hands up to her mouth, began to chew on her nails, rocked herself gently from side to side and then ran out of the nursery to hide behind the door.

"Oh Megan, please come back."

A little face peered round the door but then disappeared again.

"Megan, we thought you were really good. Wasn't she, Becky?" Liza turned to me and Megan popped her head round the door to see what I would say.

"Aye, really good. Much better than anyone in our school choir."

Liza smiled at me and nodded and with that Megan bounced back into the room. We quickly ran round her and gave her more words of praise and encouragement. However, she got no words of praise or encouragement from the choir master at her church and no offer to sing in their choir. Mrs Doherty was upset but I never saw Megan have strong emotions like a tantrum or tears. Megan never cried. Whenever something bothered her she was just the same as always, quiet like the carol she'd wanted to sing. But for Megan the music never came.

This Christmas more than any other I wanted to stay with my friends. I had no desire to go back to Ireland. I had a lot of family there but I had two special friends here who were worth more than anything. Yet my pleading to my parents never swayed them. I tried "But I'm ill" and even "If you take me I'm gonna throw up all the way there" and the words fell on deaf ears. As a last resort I even used my bedroom friends, "I can't go and leave my spiders at Christmas. It's bad manners and they'll be lonely."

Standing on the ferry as it pulled out of Holyhead docks, I thought of my other friends, Megan and Liza, and wondered what they would be doing for Christmas. Liza had wanted a bike and Megan had asked her mum to tell Santa that Megan Doherty of 42, Margaret Avenue also wanted a bike.

As for me, I always knew it was a mistake to ask Santa what I really wanted as I certainly would not receive it. Instead Leah always got what I had asked for, so we'd have an even bigger excuse to argue with each other. I had the distinct feeling that Santa knew mother very well, in fact I would go so far as to say they were probably the same person. I had no idea where my father fitted in - probably one of Santa's helpers, an insignificant elf.

We had borrowed a car from Tony Quinn. My father was the only one who could drive; he said he would never let mother behind the wheel of a car as he had no smart suits to go to court in and inquests were so long and boring. He drove all the way to Holyhead where we finally caught the ferry to Dublin. True to my word, I managed to vomit the entire way and really annoyed Peter and Leah who had to sit next to me in the car.

On the ferry, mother thought it best if I got some fresh air and then went to the cabin to get some sleep as we would be up most of the night travelling. I actually preferred sailing in the night than during the day, but who was I to have an opinion? The parents went to one of the restaurants while Peter and Leah went to the on-board cinema and I remained alone in the cabin allocated to the children. The parents had a cabin to themselves. I lay in the small rectangular cabin on the bottom bunk. It was hard and cold and the white starched sheet didn't cover the rough beige blankets that scratched my chin as I pulled them close around me.

I kept the light on and watched my coat on its hanger rock side to side, flickering the light in and out, in and out. I fell asleep in the cold, lonely cabin and when I awoke we were in Ireland - the Free State.

—EIGHT—

When we arrived in Dublin, Ireland was just the same as I remembered it. The rain poured and more rottenness was on the way. Ireland, the ends of the Earth or a piece of Heaven in the Irish Sea, depending on which side you belonged. A vast emptiness set in an emerald jewel of wildness. A paradise for the soul that seeketh freedom. Ireland. It was home but I just wished that it was for Megan and Liza too.

All the family was there, including cousins I had never seen before and others all claiming to be related in some way or another. Father said that one of them was a shit shoveller from Donegal, but I never found him or smelled him for that matter. Travelling in the car had brought back memories of days spent alone while Peter and Leah were at school, my life at the mercy of Aunt Siobvon and her tyrannical crusade upon my mind in the name of education. Aunt Siobvon and Miss Pike must have been twins separated at birth, both as humanitarian as Hitler. They differed in physical appearance, the one tall, thin and miserable-looking and the other small, fat and miserable-looking. Genghis Kahn and Vlad the Impaler, two people who had a profound place in my childhood. It is a mystery to me that I remained sane.

As the mountains and sea drifted into sight, heralding the county I had known for the first seven years of my life, even though I had been away from it for only six months I felt like a stranger now. I had seen new places, and as much as I disliked that town with its factories and grey streets I still felt peace there. Father had once said to me, on one of his more serene days, that it is people who make a place - family makes a home and friends make you welcome.

Beaulieu, our house and Great-Grandpa's pride and joy, stood majestically in the shadow of a mountain that had its base firmly rooted in the sea. Numerous cars were parked in the driveway and father moaned that at least Siobvon could have saved a place for us; mother snapped at him to shut up. I wished Christmas would hurry up as the Christmas Miracle was wearing off already.

Genghis Kahn was waiting for us at the door with the words, "I expected you over an hour ago, Sean. It's just like you to take your time and keep people waiting."

"Merry Christmas, Siobvon," replied father and kissed her on the cheek. Mother just smiled and walked on into the house.

Aunt Siobvon stared at Peter, Leah and me and announced, "There's no rooms left now but I've managed to keep Peter's old room. We put three beds in there so you're all together." Her voice was so cold that I was sure snow would follow. Aunt Siobvon had taken it upon herself to organise the whole event; she was in charge of the catering, entertainment and the general run of the household. No-one had asked her to do this, it just gave her a great amount of pleasure ordering everyone about.

The house was alive with people, like a miniature town all under cover. Father was talking to someone and mother was somewhere else. I couldn't recognise any familiar faces but Peter and Leah spotted a group of children out at the back and ran to them.

I chose to explore the house. I drifted up the stairs and no-one seemed to notice I wasn't around. I strayed down the hallway looking at the rooms, trying to remember which one was mine, but instead I found Peter's and silently walked in. I remembered the creaking floorboard. Typical. I could recall that but not where my own bedroom was. Three beds, Peter's old bed dominating the room, and bunk beds shoved in the corner like they were not welcome.

I lay down on Peter's bed and breathed in the dull silence. I could hear the noises from downstairs wafting up through walls, ceilings and floors, the muffled voices of false compliments and cold greetings of a family with so many secrets. I stared at the ceiling, remembering Peter's room well as I had often hidden in here to escape Aunt Siobvon and her ruler. Strangely, I could not remember mother having such a presence as Aunt Siobvon. Mother took Peter and Leah to school and was away for the most of the day; she said she was visiting friends but I never knew she had any. I fell asleep and was only awakened by Leah shaking me.

"C'mon on, get up."

"What? What for?" I rubbed my eyes and stumbled out of bed.

"We're going to church."

"But it's the middle of the night."

"Aren't you bloody quick? Why do you think it's called Midnight Mass?"

"Do we have to?"

"Aye." Seeing how tired and pale I looked, Leah added, "C'mon, I'll let you wear my scarf."

"The one with the reindeer on?"

"Aye."

"Thanks, Leah."

Still half asleep, I plodded downstairs with my big sister holding my hand. Aunt Siobvon was at the bottom of the stairs wrapped up in a fluffy coat.

"There you are. You're exactly like your father, you have to keep people waiting and worrying."

We followed her out and Leah wrapped her new reindeer scar round me. The driveway was alive with lights from cars, then one by one they drove away and we trundled along the mountain side. It wasn't that far to the church, basically just round the corner, but the journey that night seemed long and tiresome. I thought of the Blessed Virgin and her journey. Perhaps it felt the same as this, so long, too bloody long, a never-ending hell with turning roads that lead to nowhere. Then when she did reach the end she was told there was no room left. Finally when her son was born there was still no room left for him in men's hearts.

I gazed out of the car window and strained my eyes to see the stars but all I could see was a very bright one hovering over the mountains. Sea, mountains and sky seemed to be connected, the one feeding into the other as indigo sky trickled down onto the mountains turning them black, which in turn poured itself into the sea. Some clouds danced across the moon, yet when reflected in the sea the moon danced as well. It swayed to a rhythm but I didn't hear any music.

At last we reached the church. It was tall, towering and terrifying against the deep darkness of mountains and heavens. The car park was full and the lights of flickering candles streamed out of the huge wooden doors. It was still and silent inside. I felt as though I were in a dream. Gold, splendour and coldness merged in one enormous lie. The wooden benches creaked as everyone sat down and listened to the old tale, people listening with open eyes yet with minds somewhere else. They had come because they were expected to, because this was the only truth known and nothing else confronted that.

I turned to my father as he wriggled in his seat. I knew he didn't want to be here. He wanted to be anywhere except here. His eyes wandered helplessly around the church, from people's faces to walls to paintings to the ceiling, anywhere except to the cross. He could not look upon it or upon the wooden painted statue of the Blessed Virgin. The priest in all his fine noble splendour rambled on, re-telling the tale of so long ago about a man and his wife travelling many roads to reach a place the man called home. When they finally arrived they found nothing waiting for them – I understood that. How hopeless the man seemed, he never got anything right.

Later the adults went to the priest to take a sip of wine and a piece of bread, while the children went up to the front to see the statuesque nativity display. All around the gentle baby in his crib were animals staring at the wonder of this scene, as men kneeling down in rich clothes offered presents of frankincense, gold and myrrh. Shepherds stood behind the rich men, their flocks watching the scene with the same awe. On either side of the babe were his Earthly parents, his mother the holy vessel and Joseph. I wondered what part Joseph had to play in this drama, what right this man had to be so close to innocence and truth? I held onto my father's hand then slept the rest of the way home and only woke up when I heard Peter and Leah hurriedly fumbling about.

It was Christmas morning and I wondered what Santa had got wrong this year.

"Hey Shitty, aren't you getting up to open your presents?"

"No."

"Oh Christ, you're bloody happy, aren't you?"

"Shhh, be quiet Leah."

Leah tutted as she went out of the bedroom. Her dressing gown swished behind her.

"Are you still tired, Becky?"

"Yeah. What time is it? "

"Half-five."

"WHAT?"

Peter smiled. "Well, I'm dying to see what I've got."

"Aren't we all? But I'm not getting up at five in the morning. I'm off back to sleep."

"Okay, do you want me to open your presents for you?"

"No thanks, I can manage quite well when I get up."

"Right ye are. I was just thinking of ya. See ya later."

And off Peter bounced out of the door. I snuggled down into my warm, soft bed but was disturbed only two seconds later by Peter again as he popped his head round the door.

"Oh, by the way, merry Christmas, Becky."

Finally I woke up and, still feeling tired, I lay in Peter's bed. He had graciously let me have his as he didn't want to miss the opportunity of sleeping in a bunk bed - the top bunk, that is, after he and Leah had fought for the grand prize with everything they could lay their hands on including me. Peter won the top bunk and Leah took second place. I didn't mind. I preferred sleeping in a bed of my own, safe in the knowledge that big sister Leah was not sleeping above me. I had visions of her jumping up and down on the bunk bed and coming right through to land on my face.

I sensed that it was late morning. It was so quiet upstairs that one would have thought there was no-one in the house if not for the screams, giggles and gasps of wonder pulsating from downstairs. I felt compelled to see my present; I had to see what Santa had deliberately got wrong this time. I had asked for a bike like my soul mates back home; bikes had been very popular this Christmas judging by the number of bells tinkling. I trotted downstairs still in my pyjamas complete with hair sticking up and eyes half closed, and wandered into the huge living room adorned with an equally huge Christmas tree, its needles already falling. Wrapping paper was strewn madly across the floor and Aunt Siobvon was fussing around clearing it up, folding the paper carefully to be used again.

Father sat at one end of the sofa next to some sort-of-uncles while mother sat on one of chairs next to the fire chatting to some sort-of-cousins. My father looked at me.

"Well, hello there, sleepy head. Did you have a good night's rest? "

"It was alright." I replied, rubbing my eyes.

Aunt Siobvon turned round but regretted it.

"Goodness gracious me, just look at the state of you. You look like you've gone ten rounds with the Evil One." My strange dreams often felt like that. "And you're late, everybody's opened their presents."

Mother got up from her chair and walked across the room declaring, "She'll always be late. She'll never be early for anyone except herself." She continued to walk to the door and on outside where Peter and Leah played on their new bikes. My eyes wandered round for my present as father got up and went to the tree. There were just two presents left, a small square one and a large rectangular one. Father picked up the small one.

"Here you are, Rebekah. Merry Christmas."

Somehow I had the distinct feeling it wasn't a bike. I opened it up and beheld three books: The Railway Children, Animal Stories and Little Women. My acting skills were superb; I think I would even have convinced myself had it not been for the fact that I dropped the books on the floor when Aunt Siobvon handed me her present. The long rectangular box gave it away - a porcelain doll with a face so clear that its features were mesmerising. She wore a beautiful emerald green and gold crinoline dress with matching bonnet placed eloquently over thick ginger hair.

I thanked Auntie and declared that I had already thought of a name for her, then proceeded to take my books and my Megan upstairs out of harm's way of Peter and Leah. They knew to stay clear of any toy Aunt Siobvon had given me, though. I had once heard Auntie tell them that if they so much as touched any doll of mine, especially ones she had given me herself, then their lives would not be worth living.

Just before dinner we made our way once again to the church. Father didn't bother to come. I have no idea how he slimed his way out of it as Aunt Siobvon was stricter on that matter than the Pope. The priest babbled on about the poor, the needy and the starving, then drank wine from a gold cup.

In the evening the whole family gathered round in little groups, Aunt Siobvon closest to the blazing fire with her husband Uncle Danny beside her. Uncle Danny was a strange character; he hardly ever said anything except to bring Aunt Siobvon back down to earth again. Father sat near them. Mother was somewhere else - the Christmas Miracle was wearing off.

"Where are you thinking of going on holiday this year, Siobvon?" my father asked. Eager to boast, Aunt Siobvon came up with, "We're thinking about a cruise on the Nile." Uncle Danny looked up.

"Oh," continued my father, who seemed very interested in a thread on his Arran jumper. "Well, wherever you go I hope it will be lovely."

"Aye," Uncle Danny murmured. "The nearest pub always is."

Aunt Siobvon had made impact once again with the earth, resulting in a razor sharp stare at Uncle Danny. Father looked up with a smile in his eyes though his mouth didn't show it. Uncle Danny's eyes twinkled like the devil he was while Aunt Siobvon went from pink to red to purple so fast I thought she was going to explode.

My family. Just as with every family there were secrets, and I knew they were my father's. I was spellbound by it all, yet when I found out I was ashamed to have ever called him my father. One evening, I managed to overhear something.

While everyone was getting ready for bed, Peter and Leah were having a pillow fight. Seeing that I did not want to take part, they chased me out screaming and yelling and what followed was a sort of hide-and-seek. It was while I was hiding that I managed to overhear something my father was saying to Aunt Siobvon and other relatives who were complete strangers to me. One of my uncles asked if anyone had heard of Maggie lately. I heard my father's voice.

"I haven't seen her for ages, Jack. She keeps herself to herself and that's the way I prefer it. Though I have seen her wandering around the docks."

"Tut, it's amazing that our family could produce something like that." This low boring voice came from Aunt Siobvon. There was no mistaking her voice.

"It's such a shame about her, though," said an uncle.

"Yes, it is," came a chorus of voices.

"Say, does she still live in that very same house?"

"Aye, she still does. It's an old ruin now but she's still there. Sure, nobody sees her unless she goes for a walk round the docks, that's when I've mainly seen her. She only goes walking in the dead of night. But she knows better to stay away from me and my house."

"She should have stayed in that institution. At least she was well looked after in there."

"I know, Siobvon, but she had a right to come back into the world again. Besides, Mr McEnfry at the corner shop takes her all the things she needs, so really she has no need to come out."

The message in the bottle had been washed upon the shore. It lay there desperate to be opened and read. That night I lay in bed thinking who father and Aunt Siobvon were talking about. Who was Maggie? And which house did Maggie live in? One thing I knew for sure, I simply could not wait to get back to Megan and Liza.

—NINE—

It was the first week of the New Year. I remember an old saying that whatever you do in the first couple of weeks of a new year you will spend the rest of the year doing. That first week was full of fear, curiosity, shock and bewilderment. The following New Year I would think back and realise that the saying was true. Christmas came and went, the Miracle wore off and my parents' hearts froze again. Time went by so quickly that I think on the path of growing up I lost some days of childhood, as if they had been swept under the carpet like dirt.

When we finally arrived back from Ireland I managed to stay in the house for ten minutes then dived round to see Megan. Liza was there playing with Megan's new toys and Megan was playing with Liza's new teddy bears, so at least Santa had got something right. I desperately wanted to tell them what I had heard but felt I should acknowledge their presents first. It was Liza who brought the subject up for me.

"Have you been inside the haunted house?"

"Yes. Why do you ask? "

"What, all round it?"

"Well, I think so."

"And Megan? Has she been all round the haunted house? "

"NO!"

"Why, what else is there to see?"

"A lot more, Miss Rebekah Doen."

"I don't want to go back in that house. It's haunted."

"That was just Megan."

"I know."

"Besides, there's nothing in that house except ghosts." It was nice of her to put it so bluntly.

"Look, you two, I've got something really weird to tell you. Something I overheard while I was in Ireland."

"You can tell us after we've been to the haunted house. It won't take long and we want to let you in on our little secret."

Megan giggled, though her giggle sounded more like full scale laughter. I agreed as I was fascinated by the house. I still hadn't told Liza or Megan about the curtains falling back or the shadows I had seen at the windows, but soon everything was to fall into place. As we made our way there our feet crunched on the light snow that thinly covered the ground. Liza walked first, Megan marched after her with arms flapping beside her like a soldier, and I followed behind them ever careful where I trod as I did not want to waste the snow.

We knocked at the door, which must have been repaired. Strange though, I had not seen anybody fixing it. And I also thought it weird to knock at a house where no-one was living. Liza walked on in and Megan bounced after her.

"Shut the door, Becky."

"Why?"

"Because we don't wanna let the heat out."

"What?"

"Sh… shut doooor Bekeee!"

I shut the door and walked into the house, which did not appear to be as haunted in the daytime as it had been in twilight. The sun beams outside reflected off the snow and came in through the windows, then graced the tops of tables and wooden cabinets, exposing the dust and dirt there.

There seemed to be a warmth coming from somewhere. Liza and Megan walked on in the direction of the warmth and I followed ever obediently. We came to a room that was different to the rest. It had obviously been taken care of for it was not as dusty as the other rooms in the house. This room was full of trophies, stacks and stacks of trophies and medals. I wanted to look closer at them but Megan and Liza both ushered me on. Then Liza opened the door to a kitchen and there sat an old lady with a shawl wrapped round her, in front of a fire.

The kitchen was small compared to the rest of the house and in it were just tables and chairs and an old sofa. In one corner was some sort of shrine on a little table. The flickering flames of candles lit the old black and white pictures that surrounded it with a shimmering glow of warmth. A bunch of flowers and old tickets for buses and the cinema lay there, disregarded yet respected.

I didn't know if what I saw before me was some kind of ghost and it was not until she spoke to Megan and Liza that I realised this sight was real. I came in slowly and quietly closed the door behind me, turning round again to see Liza give her a hug while Megan had already pulled up a chair by the fire, as close to the lady as she could get.

"Becky Doen, this is Maggie. I bet you thought no-one lived here, eh? I bet you thought this place was haunted. Well, as you can see, it ain't." Liza winked knowingly.

"All th… those mmmedals are Maggie's!"

"Yeah, that's right. We've always known this place was never haunted. We used to come here often to visit Maggie. She always made us welcome."

Secrets again surrounded me. Then Maggie seemed to come out of her vacant stare.

"Doen. Did you say Doen?"

Liza looked a little uncomfortable. "Yes, Maggie. This is Re-bekah Doen."

Maggie jumped up from her chair. Megan leaned back as if to ask if we should go but I couldn't see Liza's expression as Maggie was now standing in front of me, peering into my face.

"Are you any relation to Sean Doen?"

"Yes ma'am, he's my father." I struggled to get the words out for fear of what she would do if I answered wrongly. Suddenly, Maggie grabbed me and pushed me towards the shrine; I quickly glanced at Megan who was standing up holding on to the chair. I turned my face again and found that I was nearly upon the shrine. It was dominated by old black and white photos.

"Look closer at the pictures, Miss Rebekah Doen. You'll be surprised who you can find in a photo."

Maggie's hands tightened their grip on me and I was shoved forward. I was expected to find faces in old photos, faces that no longer existed as time wipes childhood away. There was a brother and sister, the girl taller with her little brother holding her hand proudly. In some of the photos they were with their parents. I breathed in the family, fascinated by the little boy. I felt I knew him. I thought I knew him.

My father. And the parents were my grandparents.

I turned round quickly to the woman. "You're Maggie. You're Maggie."

She nodded her head like a toddler.

Liza came up to me and placed her hand on my shoulder. "I thought you knew about your auntie?" I took a good look at her. Her hair looked as if it hadn't been brushed in years, her clothes were dirty and her slippers had holes in them. This was my auntie.

She began to sing. "You're Maggie! You're Maggie!" Then she started skipping round the room. Megan looked at Liza.

"We have to go now, Maggie," Liza's voice was calm, "but we will be back again soon." Maggie appeared not to listen. She was too busy dancing round the kitchen as Liza ushered Megan out. All this was done in silence.

Standing outside on the crisp snow, I wondered what to do. I had so many questions but there was no-one whom I could ask. Father was probably gone by now on a fishing trip and I feared what mother would say. But what could she say? Everything was out. The secret. One secret, at least, was now out in the open.

My mind raced over everything until a thought struck.

"How did Megan know about Suki's plans to explore the house? I didn't know Megan then so I couldn't have told her."

"Ma... Maggie!"

"Yeah, that's right. Maggie overheard what you were gonna do so she told Megan."

"I alwaaays go t... to see M... Maggie!"

"Why didn't you say anything?"

Megan shrugged her shoulders. "Th... Tho... Thought you know!"

"Yeah! We thought you knew but just didn't want to talk about it. That's all."

"Why wouldn't I wanna talk about my mad auntie living in a derelict house?"

"Sh... She's not m... ma... mad, Bekeee. She's ju... ju... just diffrunt!"

I looked at Megan. I couldn't answer that. There was nothing to say. She had said it all.

As we walked back to Megan's house, the heavy smell of roast meats cooking filled our lungs. The scent mingled with the damp air of a bright January Sunday morning. The lighter, sweet smell of fried onions ready for the juice of cooked flesh signified that dinners were nearly ready. We opened Megan's front door to see Mrs Doherty bringing some toys downstairs. Liza looked a little puzzled when she saw her with a bundle of toys and books in her arms.

"Going somewhere?"

"No, but you lot are. You're always upstairs in that nursery so I've put some sun loungers outside for you all. Our patio has caught the sun and it will do you the world of good to get some fresh air." What Mrs Doherty really meant was 'I want you all out of the house because I'm cleaning for Britain.' We glanced at one another and agreed that adults have some strange ideas, but followed Mrs Doherty out and sank onto the loungers, immersed in our own thoughts.

It was hard to believe that Megan had kept such a secret as this from me but I don't think she actually realised what she'd done. Nothing much bothered Megan and she had no concept of time. She lived every day for itself and never made plans or looked to the future, whereas Liza was always looking forward to the time when she would be old enough to leave school. She couldn't wait to grow up. It was an unusually mild day. The sun was shining and we watched little wisps of white clouds dart across a blue meadow sky. I knew Liza was thinking deeply to herself as I could see her frowning, then she smiled to herself.

"Look how quickly the Earth is moving."

"How d... dooo you know?" bellowed Megan's deep voice.

"Just look at how fast the clouds are moving."

We saw them sweep across the sky like they were all in a race to somewhere unknown. We marvelled at the world, how fast things were happening as the Earth spun round. We had no idea that it was the wind blowing the clouds.

"What's wrong, Becky?"

"Nothing."

"Pleeese!"

I smiled at Megan. "I wish my father was here." I knew he had gone. I just knew. And I really wanted him.

"Is he working?"

"Yeah." Or just forever leaving.

"You don't like working?"

"No."

"W… Why?"

"I miss him."

"But you spent Christmas with him."

"So?"

"Well, it's better to be thankful that you spent Christmas with him than not see him at all."

"But…"

"But what?"

"Well, I never really saw him that much at Christmas. There were so many people there and he was always talking with them. He didn't really spend that much time with me, or any of us for that matter."

"At least y… you g… g… got a D… Daddy!"

"Yeah," Liza added.

"Yeah, but have I really? I never see him, he's never home and when he does come home we never talk."

"Yes you do. He took you to get your school uniform, didn't he? "

"Only `cause he had to."

"And he t… toook you ffffishin!"

"Only `cause he felt guilty for not meeting me from school on my first day."

"No, it wasn't out of guilt."

"How do you know?"

"Look Becky, parents have to work."

"Yeah, but do they always have to leave?"

Liza didn't answer and neither did Megan. They just looked up at the sky. The clouds were still racing and so was my mind.

"And look at this now."

"W… What?"

"Look where?"

"Maggie."

"Oh!"

"Becky, if we'd known we wouldn't have taken you to see her. We honestly thought you knew. You went along with the haunted house tale for so long that we thought you were protecting Auntie Maggie."

"My father didn't even tell me he had a sister, let alone she lived up the street from me. Besides, he has nothing to do with her. If you knew who I was and who she was, why the hell didn't you tell me?"

"We honestly thought you knew. After we saw your father mend the door we thought everything was out in the open. We just thought you didn't want to talk about it. And you wanted to stay away from her."

"My father mended the door?"

"Yeah."

"When?"

"After it f… f… fell off!"

"After you'd been exploring with the Pink Brigade."

"That long ago? Why couldn't someone have told me?"

"Well, it's not just your dad's fault, Peter knew too. That's why we thought you must have known as well."

"What?!"

"Peter h… help m… mend doooor!"

"I can't believe this."

"Sorry, Becky."

"S… Sooory!"

"Oh, it's not your fault. It's my bloody family."

"So it's okay?"

"Yeah, it's okay."

But it wasn't okay. Once again I was the last to know. I always came last, even with my father, it seemed. I longed to see him now just to talk about his sister, Maggie. But he was hardly ever home and I knew I wouldn't see him much after Christmas. I kept quiet about Maggie with mother; I couldn't stand her going on about it. Yet both Peter and Leah knew.

"What, you didn't know we've got a crazy auntie?"

"She's not crazy, Leah."

"No, she just belongs to this family. Says it all really, doesn't it?"

"That's not fair."

"No it isn't, but what can we do about it?"

"We could invite her to tea?"

"Are you mad? Better watch out, little sister, you'll be next to get it. Don't you know it runs in the family?"

With that Leah scrambled out of the door. The silence between us was as wide as the secrets in our family. Like the pictures of Maggie and my father, a sister and brother, snatched moments of life the same as the snatched moments of conversations I had with my own brother and sister.

—TEN—

Father decided not to come home for half-term. I wondered what he was hiding from this time; there was definitely something keeping him away. If it was Maggie then why had he decided to move here, with her living just up the street, her house dominating the entire avenue? It seemed that he was ashamed of her yet he had defended her to Aunt Siobvon and mended the door. It was a mystery to me.

But in those days I had Liza, school and Megan. There was so much going on out of school that nothing mattered much there, but I was always happy to go and relish in the antics that Nigel and Billy got up to.

After the hair-on-fire episode Nigel had not been allowed anywhere dangerous, so in the cookery lessons he was only allowed to wash up. However, this did not prevent the Black Group – or, as Miss Pike called us, the Evil Team - from having our fun. One day while we were making pastry, the cookery teacher Mrs Lacy was called out of the classroom for an urgent telephone call. As no cookers were on she felt she could leave us for a few moments. Big mistake.

As soon as she was gone, Billy jumped up and grabbed some of the pastry she'd been showing us how to make, rolled it up into a little ball and threw it at Nigel who had his back to us. As the pastry ball hit him he turned round and his eyes fell straight on Billy. The class began to get a little nervous and a puny boy called Phillip Mathewson, whose parents were both lawyers and whom we took very little notice of, turned to Billy and said, "I say, why don't you stop that and grow up."

So naturally Nigel grabbed a flour bag and proceeded to throw it over Phillip Mathewson, declaring "It's snowing!" Phillip looked like a snowman, his eyelashes flickering with the snow flour on them, and everybody in the class began to giggle. Billy had made more ammunition for himself and another pastry ball hit Nigel. This was now war.

Nigel quickly ran to the `fridge, took out the eggs at speed and threw them at Billy. Everyone started to move out of the way, hysterical classmates running round the kitchen trying to hide, and when Nigel saw this his new targets were anything that moved. Eggs, flour and Mrs Lacy's special pastry were all now being used in this bloody war, and Liza and I joined our side - the side with the ammunition, that is.

Suki was screaming as if she'd been mortally wounded. For some reason she had been allowed to wear a pink dress to school that day, but now regretted it. Her hair and pretty pink-ribboned dress looked like some kind of cake mixture. It was not until we saw everyone standing still, huddled in a corner with frightened faces, that we realised Mrs Lacy had returned. We turned round slowly to see Mr 'Well Well' Lukas too. We hadn't seen him since that very first day back from the summer holidays. As far as we believed he lived in his office, never coming out and never going in. He just sort of appeared and disappeared. He seemed to be some sort of divine entity that we knew existed but never saw except on very rare occasions. Sometimes we respected him and sometimes we didn't, but we knew he existed; it was a bit like God, we just weren't sure.

However, on this occasion we did respect him. He never uttered a word, merely pointed to the door, and we silently walked like lambs to the slaughter past Mrs Lacy who gave us a curious look. Still Mr Lukas did not say a word. It was not until we reached the corner of the corridor that we heard Mrs Lacy scream when she saw her beloved classroom with her beloved pastry now plopping off walls, cookers, `fridges and our classmates.

Fun had its price. We got three weeks' detention plus a recommendation that the Black Team be split up the following September; but that was a long way off so we just forgot about it.

I hated coming home late from school. The extra hour at school could have been spent with Megan, Liza and Aunt Maggie.

I found out that Aunt Maggie was not crazy, just different like Megan had said. She was proud of her shining accomplishments and I helped her polish her trophies and medals. She would tell me stories about Ireland and swimming in the great ocean. I could relate to it. I realised that she was a source of embarrassment to the family just because of her differences, but she didn't appear crazy to me. Her hair was crazy, yes, but maybe she liked the wild look?

There were days when she did not want to speak and days when she never stopped talking. One subject might produce a sensitive and emotional response, while on other days the same subject yielded a rather cold and disinterested response. I learned to take one day at a time with Auntie. In later years I would realise what a valuable lesson this had been. Sometimes she would ask how father was, how was the fishing and did he still have "that old trawler". I had only known of one since I was born, so I answered in the positive.

It was some time before I actually told my father that I knew. Although Peter and Leah had known for quite a while, they knew it was a sore point between my parents so they kept it secret. Always secrets. Why had I never been told that I had an auntie? Why was I never told that some people are different? Secrets and sorrows had created my family. Auntie had seen and known institutions, special schools and psychiatric hospitals. But if only members of the family had tried to understand her or had tried to befriend her, they would have realised that her sensitivity and changing moods were not the stuff of dark sorrows and hidden secrets. It was simply a case of her being that way.

Liza enjoyed her company and Megan liked her too. Megan thought her little habits and the way she lived her whole life were funny. How she lived in just one room of the house, her bed opposite the kitchen table. How she had a shrine in the corner full of old bits and pieces, old photos, old bus and cinema tickets. Old memories now reawakened by new questions from her niece.

I was intrigued to know more about my auntie, of course, and I longed to talk to my father about his sister. Why had she gone away? How did she know me? Where had she gone to? Why was she given this house? How long had she stayed away? These were questions that never let me rest, going over and over in my brain all night and most of the day. At least at school the antics the Black Team got up to would dull the questions, but as soon as the home bell rang they would spring back into my mind. Then I thought about asking Liza. She might know why.

"Do you know anything about Auntie?" Auntie seemed a perfectly good name to use as Liza and Megan had also both taken her into their hearts as their own auntie long before she had entered mine.

"What like?"

"Well, where she lived before she came here?"

"Oh no, not really. I've only ever known her from here."

"So you have no idea how she got here, then?"

"In a car, probably." Liza's sarcasm raised its head again and I knew any attempt to extract information from her would be fruitless. But once, while playing in Megan's house, she did say something that began to form an outline of Auntie's life. Megan had just declared we should play doctors and nurses.

"Let's play hospitals instead," Liza added.

"Yeah."

"Okaaay!"

"Yeah, hospitals where they tie mad people up to the wall, like the one Auntie Maggie went to."

"My auntie never went to one of them," I said protectively.

"Oh, yes she did. My dad said she went to the nut house."

"Why?"

"I don't know why but that's where she's been. Then they let her out and she came to live here."

"But why?"

"Oh Becky, don't ask me, I don't know. You ask too many ruddy questions."

"Well, I'm not playing nut house. You're not strapping me to any wall."

"And meee!"

In the end we played with the dolls' house. Liza probably forgot all about it but I carried it within for a long time. I thought that knowing something about my auntie's whereabouts would have answered some questions, yet in the end it only brought up more. Like, why had she been sent to a mental institution? What had she done wrong? Who had sent her away? So many secrets. Maybe I should have just accepted the secrets and lived with them like the rest of the family but I could not. I was different. To me, secrets seemed to be just lies in a trinket box of words.

It was Peter who gave me the first clue, which led to many others. He caught me coming out of Auntie's house.

"Hey squirt, what ya doing in there? You know it's haunted."

Feeling smug, knowing something he knew, I replied, "I've just been to see our Auntie."

"Nutty Maggie?" I looked sharply at him. "Oh, don't worry, I won't tell Pa that his favourite knows the secret."

"How long have you known?"

"Forever. She used to live with us in Ireland until she nearly... well, I mean until she wasn't there." Peter felt awkward. I could sense him trying to find some phrase that would explain everything. I could see by the way his body moved like a snake from side to side that he felt uncomfortable. He had said something he shouldn't have. I stepped silently towards him and stood looking up at my big brother.

"What?" I almost whispered.

"Tut. `Tis nothing. Get away from me, squirt. I'm off out with the guys."

He pushed me aside and ran down the street out of sight. I kicked the ground and wandered silently back home.

I had begun to realise that my absences were greatly appreciated and, when I did appear, I wasn't exactly welcome. The others' attitude towards me mirrored their attitude towards my father, as my actions mirrored those of my father. He would spend all his time away, working. I would also try to be out of the house more often than I was in.

Of course, when father came back at the beginning of March he wasn't going to stay long. So I had to tell him quickly and when he was on his own; now I was creating my own secrets. I figured that while he was getting the ship ready for its next voyage was the best time.

"I know about Maggie."

"What? Who told you?"

"No-one, I found it out myself. It wasn't that hard. She only lives up the street."

"Listen, Rebekah, you stay away from her." He stared at me.

"Why?"

"Because she's dangerous."

"She's harmless."

"My God, I knew it was a mistake to come back here. Your mother's responsible for this."

"No-one's responsible."

"Does your mother know?"

"Nobody knows. Only you, but you've always known."

"Rebekah, please."

"Please what?"

"Don't go near her."

"Why?"

"She's different."

"What's wrong with being different?"

He didn't answer. Meaningless words were all we ever said to one another. I stood on the dock and watched his ship drift out of sight, wondering when I would see my father again.

One day after school, Liza was going relative-visiting and Megan was going to church, father was away and my mother, brother and sister were unbearable. I slammed the door on my way out, declaring I'd be back when I'm back. I knew they wouldn't be bothered. I wandered to Auntie's.

"Hello, Becky."

"Hello, Auntie."

She seemed talkative.

"I'm gonna clean my trophies. How about you?"

"We only cleaned them yesterday."

"Dust collects quickly."

"All right."

She got her polish and two dusters and handed me one. "Good day at school, Becky?" She was talkative!

"Yeah. No worse than normal."

"That's good."

I fought back my curiosity about what happened in between her living with us in Ireland to living in a mental hospital, feeling I should first start a congenial conversation. Enquires should have a firm base.

"Did you like living in Ireland, Auntie?"

"Loved every minute of it." Well, that was a quick conversation. I tried something else.

"Did you go to church, Auntie?"

"Yes."

"I used to be drag… I went with Aunt Siobvon."

"She's not your auntie."

A response!

"You only have one real auntie and that's me."

"Oh." She seemed to be slipping into sensitivity again but I wanted to carry on. I looked at the polished trophy in my hand. "Do you like swimming, Auntie?" A smile released her tension.

"There's nothing quite like it. The sense of freedom and purity." Strange words, but this was Auntie Maggie.

"Did you swim in the sea in Ireland?"

"I did."

"Do you remember the steps going down to the sea?"

The trophy went through the window. Auntie began mumbling to herself, oblivious now to my presence.

"Baby fell in water. Baby ran down steps. Baby shouldn't be in water."

"Baby? What baby?"

"I was just going down to swim. The door didn't shut, baby ran after me. Baby ran into water."

"What baby? Auntie, what baby?"

"I jumped in and saved baby Becky. I didn't try to drown her. I'm not responsible. It was an accident."

"What?! Auntie, I'm okay."

"Baby's okay, Siobvon. Don't send me away."

"Siobvon sent you away because you saved my life?"

"Sean never did anything to help me."

"Auntie Maggie, it's okay. It's over. I'm sorry. I'm so sorry." I put my hand on Auntie's shoulder. She was kneeling down crying in the corner, still clutching the duster and saying over and over again, "Don't send me away. Don't send me away."

"It's alright, Auntie. I won't send you away. I'll never send you away." I sat down beside her and stroked her wild hair away from her eyes. I put my head on her shoulder. "What would we do without you?"

Auntie was still now. I had her attention. "Who couldn't do without me?"

"Well, Megan, Liza and me of course. Auntie, why on Earth would I send you away when I've only just met you? I don't want to lose you again."

She was calm now as she began to speak more softly.

"It was an accident, Rebekah Doen. You ran ahead. I did not push you in. I tried to save you."

"I know. I know. It's okay. I'm still here aren't I?"

"You don't hate me, then?"

"Auntie, I could never hate you. You saved my life despite what the others have said."

I wondered if she realised the hatred that surrounded her, the fear and embarrassment she brought to members of the family with her mood swings and her sensitivity. Perhaps she was like Megan, so far into her own world that she never quite knew what was happening on the outside so-called real world. I think there were times I would have liked to dive into Megan's world, to be locked away from it all. Yet perhaps Auntie was aware of the hatred and others' lack of understanding, the embarrassment she caused her brother, my father. In later years, when the tide of time had swept over us all, he still could not say, "This is my sister, Margaret Rose Doen." Poor father.

The next time I saw father, I said nothing of what I knew. I did not even ask him how or why he could send his sister away for saving my life. But I now understood more about my family, even if it did hurt.

—ELEVEN—

The coming of spring brought with it Easter and the `flu. The town had a so-called epidemic on its hands, and even pharmacies ran out of aspirins and cough syrup. It seemed that every house had developed a virus that lasted for weeks, and our house was no different. First it was my turn. Father was away, naturally, so mother nursed me and I was pleasantly surprised that she made a very good nurse until Leah got it, then I had to fend for myself. After Leah, Peter decided to catch the `flu right at the beginning of the Easter holidays (what a waste of a perfectly good illness!). I had to look after him and, my God, was he pathetic.

"Oh, Becky, I can't swallow." "Oh, Becky, I can't breathe." "Becky, I'm cold." "Becky, I'm too hot." "Oh, Becky, I can't eat this." "Becky, I'm done for."

Oh brother! That Easter was one I would never forget.

Father came home for the Easter break but soon he too would fall victim to the deadly virus sweeping the town and our house. He was the type who never liked to admit they were sick, embarrassed if you told him he looked ill. But father was… well, let's just say I knew where Peter inherited his pathetic streak from. He was in such a bad mood the entire time. I was given the job of looking after him as mother said she wanted to take care of the children; that didn't bother father, who said he didn't want mother looking after him anyway because she might poison him. The conversations between mother and father were simply charming.

My father was a demanding patient. He would try to come downstairs to make his own food. Not that he ate much anyway as he had lost his appetite, but he couldn't stand up without feeling faint. Then he was hungry. Then he said he couldn't eat anything.

"Well, what do you want to eat?"

"I don't know. But I have to eat something. I have to keep my strength up."

"I'll make you a cup of tea."

"Aye, that'll do." I was half-way down the stairs when he shouted, "And bring up some bananas and ice-cream as well."

"They'll do you the world of good," I advised as I placed them on the bed.

"Aye, very good for you is bananas."

"And ice-cream?"

"Ice-cream is as well. It's perfect for the `flu as it cools you down, helps your sore throat and don't question me."

"No, of course not. Questions are forbidden. I might find something out I already know." I couldn't help myself. I just thought of Auntie Maggie all on her own. But I had struck a nerve with father; his sister was his Achilles heel.

"What the hell do you mean? You haven't seen her again have you?"

"I'll see her when I like."

"Becky, please."

"No, please. I have an auntie who saved my life and all you can do is have nothing to do with her."

"Becky, she tried to kill you."

"She saved my life."

"Becky - "

"Eat your ice-cream, it's melting. Is there anything else you would like me to bring up?"

"No. Why? "

"I'm just asking."

"Are you going out?"

"Yes."

"Where are you going?"

"To play with Megan and Liza."

"Oh!"

I wasn't, I had lied but then father had lied to me. Keeping a secret is just the same as a lie, isn't it? I stepped out of the door and walked on up to Auntie Maggie's. I would call on Megan later as both she and Liza were ill. Auntie's garden was full of yellow tulips and daffodils which seemed to soak up the warmth of the sun's rays. They swayed gently in the damp, `flu-ridden air. Auntie was in a surprisingly good mood.

"Hello, Auntie."

"Aaah, my favourite niece."

I smiled and knew how true that was. Auntie never lied to me. It was strange how everyone looked down upon Auntie and Megan, yet they were the most open and honest people I knew.

"You look very happy." Albeit with uncombed hair and clothes a mess. "How are you today, Auntie?"

"Yes. Yes. I'm very happy today, Rebekah."

"Why?"

"It's just a lovely sunny day."

"Yes, but it's very damp and the air feels heavy."

"Oh no, everything in the world is good today. How's your father, Rebekah?"

"He's ill auntie. He's got the `flu so he's ill in bed."

"Oh, my poor little brother is ill. Is he in a lot of pain?"

"No. Not that I know of, but if he was I'm sure he'd let us know."

"Well, I wonder what I could do to cheer him up?"

Fearing father's reaction to a surprise visitor, and one that he didn't even visit when he was well, I said, "Oh, there's nothing you can do, Auntie. It's just a cold after all."

"I know what I could do."

Oh God. "What?!"

"Cut him some flowers. You'd take them to him, Rebekah, wouldn't you?"

"Well yes, if you're sure, Auntie. They look so nice in the garden, though."

But it was too late. She had proceeded out into the garden armed with scissors, where she picked a beautiful bunch of flowers that I held while she cut more.

"You know, Auntie, it's a shame to cut these. I mean, they only die indoors."

"Yes, Rebekah, but they give so much joy inside. It makes me happy to see flowers inside as they bring a little piece of sunshine into any house. Flowers mean so much, Rebekah. When someone gives you flowers it shows how much they care and I would be so happy knowing Sean is looking at my flowers. It makes me happy knowing he's happy."

"Oh, Auntie Maggie!" I wanted to say, 'You fool. You really are bloody crazy if you believe that father could be happy thinking of you.' But I couldn't say that so instead I replied, "I think you've got enough flowers, Auntie. You don't need to cut any more."

"Are you sure?"

"Yes, positive. We don't have that many vases."

"Okay, well let's take them inside and see if we can find something to wrap round them."

As we went inside, I could hear her bouncing behind me. We got to the kitchen/bedroom/living room and I turned to see her standing quietly behind me, when only moments before she had been talkative. I stood waiting to see what she would do next. I didn't have to wait long. Auntie began to hum and slowly sway from side to side, rocking herself to music only she could hear. She raised her arms and swung them in the air. Her humming got louder. Her feet began to move, her arms wrapped round an imaginary partner as she began to sweep around the room with him. Her face had changed from a sweet contentment to a full exuberance and excitement. The music had got louder, with a full orchestra blazing out a song that was played just for Auntie, especially for Maggie.

I realised it was useless to stand there anymore. Auntie might go on and dance all night. As she swirled around the room, I side-stepped my way out still clutching the flowers she had cut. At the front door I put the lock on and gently pulled it to a close. On hearing the click of the lock, I knew Auntie would be safe for the rest of the night. She probably wouldn't even realise I was gone. Her orchestra would keep her busy all night and no doubt she would dance until she dropped. But as I walked down the avenue to our house, I knew that at least she was safe. As I passed Megan's house, her mother was out in the garden - cutting flowers!

"Hello, Mrs Doherty."

"Hello, Rebekah. What have you got there?"

"Some flowers Auntie Maggie cut for me to give to father. Are you cutting flowers for anyone in particular?"

"Yes, Megan. She's very ill, Becky. I worry about her so much. She's a big strong lass and everything but when she gets anything wrong with her, like measles or mumps or this `flu, she gets it ten times worse than anyone else."

"I'm sorry, Mrs Doherty. But at least the flowers will cheer her up."

"Aye. That they will. She misses not seeing you and Liza." Mrs Doherty drew close. "You know, Becky, she loves playing with you two so much."

"And Auntie Maggie?"

"Aye." Mrs Doherty smiled. "She loves that old lunatic up there. How is Maggie? I haven't seen her since Megan took ill. I haven't had the chance to go in and see how she is. I usually collect her shopping for her if Mr McEnfry can't deliver it."

"Oh, she's fine. She's full of energy today. Full of the joys of spring, you might say."

"Oh, that's grand to hear. Well, I'd better get back to Megan." Mrs Doherty turned to go back into the house.

"Mrs Doherty, if it's not too much bother, may I come back after I've taken these flowers in, to visit Megan? I won't stay long. I'd just like to see her."

"Oh Becky, that would be just grand."

"Okay. Well, I'll see you in a minute."

"Aye. I'll leave the door off the latch and you can come straight on in, alright?"

The minute I got home, I heard father shouting down the stairs.

"Where have you been?"

"Talking to Mrs Doherty." It was sort of a lie and sort of the truth, but his next query decided things for me about the flowers.

"You haven't seen that mad bitch up there, have ya?"

"No." I proceeded to the kitchen and put the flowers in a vase, then took them up to him. It gave me cruel delight that he would be looking at them.

"And where the hell are they from?"

"Mrs Doherty gave me them for you."

"Why?"

"I don't know why. She was just being nice. She was cutting some for Megan as well. She's really ill so I'm going on up to see her again."

"You're leaving me again?"

"Aye. You can sleep now. You've got everything you need." I glanced round. He had everything one needed while battling with a cold - tissues, juice, aspirins… cola? "Who brought you the bottle of cola?"

"Your mother."

"Oh, that's nice of her."

Father looked at me with disdain. "Drink some of it, will ya?"

"What! Why?"

"See if it's poisoned."

"Don't be daft."

"You think I'm kidding? Go on, there's a glass, have a drink of it."

"No, I'm not."

"Why? Do you know something I don't? "

"Look, mother wouldn't try to poison you. She'd be the obvious culprit."

"Aye." That last remark had got him thinking.

"Look, I'm going to visit Megan for a bit. Try and have a sleep."

"You would tell me, Becky, wouldn't you if you were seeing Maggie?"

I stared straight into father's eyes. "Aye, of course I would. Alright?"

"Aye, alright then."

He believed me. I was getting good at this lying game; it must be genetic. As I walked out of the door, he called after me.

"You won't forget to thank Mrs Doherty for the flowers, will ya?"

"Oh yeah, of course I will," I dutifully replied.

I walked up to Megan's house and shouted hello but no-one answered. I knew where Megan's bedroom was, it was a path I had trodden many times, so up I went. I wondered what Mrs Doherty would do if anything ever happened to Megan.

"Hello," I shouted again.

"Come on in, Becky." Mrs Doherty was bending over Megan, tucking her up in bed.

"Hi, Megan."

"He... Hello, Becky." Her voice sounded weak compared to normal and her face was a strange flustered colour. She looked so thin, I couldn't believe it was the same Megan I had seen only a week ago.

"How ya doing?"

"Not toooo g... good, Becky."

Mrs Doherty pulled up a chair for me and beckoned for me to come and sit down.

"Do you want a drink of anything, Becky?"

"No, thank you."

"Are you sure?"

"Aye, I'm fine."

Mrs Doherty turned to Megan. "Do you want anything, sweet-heart?"

"No thank, Mammy," she whispered.

"Well, okay. I'll leave you two for a bit, all right?" She went out but didn't go far; I could hear her pottering around in the nursery. I turned to Megan.

"Do you want me to do anything for you?"

"No. It g... gooood you here. I was b... bored. Mammy tr... tries so much."

"She loves you very much, Megan, that's why she fusses around you."

There was silence for a while and Megan closed her eyes.

"I have b... bad cold."

"Yes, I know. You're much more ill than I ever was with it."

Megan reached out her hand to me. It felt so feeble, I could feel the bones beneath the skin and the blue veins shone through.

"How's Liza?"

"I haven't seen her since we broke up for Easter. I was ill, remember? In the holidays we should be playing out with Auntie Maggie."

"How is she?"

"She's fine. I went to see her today and she was really happy. We went into the garden and she cut some flowers for father. He's ill too."

"Did you t... tell him fl... flowers from M... Maggie?"

"No, I told him they were from your Mammy. Is that okay?"

Megan laughed and nodded.

"Yes... Mammy un... der... stansss."

Well, at least someone does, I thought. Megan's eyes closed again. She tilted her head to one side and her hand released its grip.

"Megan, are you alright?"

"Yesss... I just t... tired, Becky."

And with that Mrs Doherty entered the room. I let go of Megan's hand, bent over and kissed her forehead as she fell back to sleep. Mrs Doherty followed me down the stairs and at the door she showed her obvious concern.

"Thank you for coming, Rebekah. Do you think Megan is really ill?"

"Well, it's just a cold, isn't it? And like you say, she gets things ten times worse than anyone else."

"Aye, you're right. I'm just worrying needlessly, aren't I?"

She closed the door behind me and no doubt hurried back upstairs to Megan's side, where she would stay all night. Megan was certainly ill and the rest of the Easter holidays would be rather eventful for us all. The next day I went to see Liza. One of her brothers opened the door, another one showed me where Liza was and another one brought Liza and me hot chocolate.

"It must be great to have these running around you for everything!"

"Yes, they're my slaves. They do anything I ask them to."

One brother who heard her reply threw a cushion at her.

"I'll leave you alone then. Don't want to listen to all your girly girly talk anyway." He wriggled his bum as he swayed out of the door and Liza threw the cushion after him. She picked up her mug of hot chocolate, then stopped and looked at me with a pathetic plea.

"Oh, stop it," I said. "You look like Peter, milking it for all its worth, aren't you?"

"Well, I might as well. It is the holidays."

I glanced round the room; the teddy bears were everywhere, even on the floor. Liza had so many in the bed with her that I was sure she'd soon have to move out to give them room.

"Are you comfortable in there?"

"Yeah, I've got all my buddies round me." She snuggled up next to her favourite, a huge giant panda.

"I went to see Megan yesterday."

She sat up. "And?"

"And she looks really ill, Liza."

Liza flopped down in the bed again. "Oh shit! She gets so ill Becky. You and I are alright in a couple of days but when Megan gets ill it lasts for ages and then she's really weak. The last time she got the measles she nearly went blind."

"Is there anything we can do?"

"No nothing. Just be there. Just be her friends."

"Aye," I softly whispered.

There was a silence between us that seemed to herald the future and what it would bring. The days were getting longer but the time spent between three friends was getting shorter. I wonder if somehow we knew that then, sitting in Liza's bedroom worrying about Megan. The silence was broken by her front door shutting.

"I think it's Mum." Footsteps were heard coming up the stairs and the door opened.

"Hello, darling. Hello, Becky. How are you both? Do you want something to eat? "

"We'll have some of your special sandwiches."

"Alright, then. Good to see you haven't lost your appetite, Liza love."

"Of course not. God help us if she does."

Liza's mum laughed at my comment. "Absolutely. Alright then, I'll just go and do your sandwiches."

"Mum, I want to go and see Megan."

"No Liza, you're not well enough."

"But when I get better?"

"No, I don't want you going round."

"Why?"

"Because I said and that's it." Liza's mum left the room. We could hear her footsteps on the stairs sounding a little heavier going down than they had coming up.

"I'm going to see Megan, Becky, whether I'm better or not." I could see Liza biting her lip. She was spinning the idea of how to see Megan round in her head. "I know, I can tell Mum I'm going to see Aunt Maggie instead. I can get away with that, can't I? You'll stick up for me, won't you? "

"Oh, sure."

That's great! Now Liza's using Aunt Maggie to hide the truth about Megan from her mother. It was ironic after I'd told father I hadn't seen Maggie and instead I used Megan. By the time Liza was well enough she did go round to see Megan but Megan was so ill that Mrs Doherty wouldn't let Liza see her. So the door was firmly shut and it wouldn't be for the last time.

In the third week of the Easter holidays we saw an ambulance outside Megan's house. Late at night she was rushed to hospital with difficulty in breathing and there she stayed until the beginning of half-term. I wanted to go and see her many times but both my parents declined to take me. Father said he had a terrible fear of hospitals and couldn't bear to see people die; I told him Megan only had a bad cold but he replied "Nevertheless". At least mother never gave any bullshit excuse. She just said, "Oh, she'll be out soon. Don't fret."

"But - "

"But nothing. She's in the best place if anything happens."

"What's going to happen?"

"Nothing. Becky, don't worry, she'll be alright. You don't need to go and see her."

"Oh please, Mammy. Please take me to see Megan."

"No, Becky."

"Why?"

"Because I can't be bothered. I'm too busy just to sit there in a hospital chair. No Becky. And don't ask me again." That was mother's answer; at least it was the truth even if it did upset me.

When Megan was finally released from hospital she was very weak and had lost a lot of weight. Liza was right - when an illness finally leaves Megan it takes something from her. Measles had nearly made her blind and the `flu had nearly made her deaf. Mrs Doherty never left her daughter's side, as if she couldn't bear to be without her, as if she cherished every moment as though it would be their last.

Yes, that Easter brought a lot of differences. There was definitely a change in the air and not just the passing of seasons, the coming of another summer. This would be like no other summer.

—TWELVE—

Although I had not spent that much time with them, and indeed if I were honest I'd say I had avoided them like the plague, the Pink Brigade still regarded me as a member of their team. At school, Katie and Suki were becoming a real nuisance. Though Katie often tried to talk to me, as soon as Suki came along she would change her mind and go off with the rest of the gang. Suki had grown up faster than any of us; she began to wear make-up and care about her clothes and what she looked like. Suki's pride and joy was her golden hair, so long that it fell below her waist. She wore a plait most days when she was at school, while other days she wore it down.

The days grew longer and warmer and summer was finally here. Everyone knew that it would soon be the summer holidays and six weeks of playing. At school, the lessons were more relaxed and Miss Pike even wore a yellow dress; I was amazed by this for her normal colour was dark brown or, if she were feeling really adventurous, navy. Mrs Lacy let us make chocolate crunchies and Mr Lukas was getting ready to retire, much to the relief of Towering Inferno. However, his retirement was not actually real - Mr 'Well Well' had had a nervous breakdown. I would like to state for the record that he was not the last teacher to have a nervous breakdown after teaching us, though he was the first.

We all wondered if the proposed splitting up of our team would be remembered in the new term. However, it was and we got the news in the supposed Fun Week, the last week of term. Everyone was called into the assembly hall to be told our new classes. Teams would be sorted out when we came back but Billy and Towering Inferno were separated into different classes, while Liza and I remained in the same class though not in the same team. However, our class was the very one we were hoping to get out of. Miss Pike had requested that both Liza and I re-take the first year. Liza had 'not succeeded sufficiently' in both her Maths and Science subjects while I had to re-take because I had 'not conformed to educational requirements'. Apparently, I did not take subjects seriously and I did not complete my homework assignments, and Miss Pike said that the freedom-loving Irish in me had to be controlled if I were even 'to succeed dismally within this great education system'.

I listened, creaked my neck to the side and swallowed down a mouthful of spit. What could I do except simply accept it? We'd had had our draft papers after making a mess of the cookery classroom. No doubt Suki's mother had something to do with the severity of our punishment, though I simply cannot understand why she would make such a fuss of her daughter coming home looking like a cream cake.

We the Black Team declared that enough was enough. They were not going to push us around anymore. Drastic times called for drastic measures. We no longer did our work (not that we ever did), we were nuisances at dinner and we disturbed everyone in Assembly. Despite harsh words from Miss Pike and harsh looks from Mr Lukas, nothing could deter us from being 'pure demons' as Mrs Lacy had once called us. However, even though we had committed all these offences we were still not content that we had done justice to our jailors. We stood in the corner of the playground one morning Break with our arms crossed, attempting to look mean towards anyone who invaded our space.

"It's not fair."

"What's not fair?" enquired Billy.

"All of it."

"Oh."

Knowing my friend Billy, I guessed he was not entirely sure what we were talking about so I intervened on his behalf. "I think it's a bit harsh really to split us up."

"Oh, yeah!" The penny had dropped.

"But we're getting the best revenge possible."

"That's right. We're one hundred per cent pains in the arse now." Looking up at Towering Inferno we all nodded except Liza.

"But it still doesn't feel right. It doesn't feel enough."

"What do you mean?"

"I mean, we haven't got them where it hurts."

"Well, where does it hurt?"

"How the bloody hell do I know, Billy?"

"Yeah. What we need is something so rotten that everybody in the school will suffer as a result."

"Something that will basically scare the shit out of them."

"Yeah."

"Yeah. What?"

"Billy, why don't you use your brain?"

"Ain't got one. If I had I wouldn't be in the Black Team."

"Hey, there's nothing wrong with the Black Team."

"All I'm saying is - "

"How about a ghost?" I had been quiet so long that my team mates gave a little jump with surprise. Liza looked at me as if she knew what I was thinking. "Yeah… a ghost. We could get a ghost to haunt the school."

"Then everyone wouldn't come to school because they'd be too frightened."

"Right."

"Right. But how we gonna get a ghost to come to school?"

"We create one."

"Who's gonna believe us? We are the Black Team after all and not to be trusted."

"So how we gonna get a ghost to come here?"

"Ouija board." My conspirators looked at me once more. Billy gulped and Nigel viewed me with suspicion while Liza just looked on. "We could call one up on a ouija board," I repeated.

"How?"

"We can make one."

"How?"

"What do we have to do?"

"What do they look like?"

"We won't call up anything evil, will we?"

My friends were full of questions, their faces concerned and confused. I merely reassured them with a calming air and declared, while looking at the school and slowly nodding my head, "There are ways." My calmness silenced them but we all jumped when the bell signalled the end of playtime.

However, so eager were we that we planned and prepared every stage of the operation. We made the ouija board, which simply consisted of cut out paper, drew out letters of the alphabet and the words Yes and No. At the given time we were to borrow - well, steal - a glass from the dinner hall and that would be our pointer. The right time to perform our treason would have to be dinner time, after we had eaten of course! This didn't give us much time to get to our classroom and lay everything out; it was going to be a rush but we felt we could make it.

We chose Friday as a good day since it would give the ghosts the weekend to settle in. We did everything as planned. After our dinner we raced to the classroom, narrowly avoiding Pam the dinner lady doing her rounds of checking rooms (I think personally she just liked snooping around). We laid everything out. The letters went around the desk in a semicircle, placed the borrowed cup in the middle and on either side placed the words Yes and No. We took a deep breath and placed our index fingers on the cup. We stared at each other. None of us thought we would get this far so we had no idea what came next. Nigel looked at Billy, Billy looked at Liza and Liza looked at me.

"Well?"

As it had been all my idea I thus felt compelled to do something or start the ball rolling, so to speak.

"Ahem." My comrades stared at me. I let my mind go and suddenly... "Oh great spirits, free yourselves from the celestial plane and join us here in Miss Pikes' classroom."

Liza gazed at Nigel. Her eyes were wide as saucers and her eyebrows were touching her fringe. But I was on a roll.

"Come, o wise and ancient ones. Break through the barriers of time and space to help us, the Black Team, really give it to the rest of the school."

I opened my eyes, which had been shut for this second blast of treasonable magic. My conspirators, for the first time in their lives, were speechless. I wondered if I had overdone it and was just about to take my finger off the glass when suddenly it began to move. Billy tried to scream but no sound came from his mouth. Liza and Nigel were too scared to move and just stared in wonder as the glass moved from M to I to N to D. I whispered "Mind". The pointer then moved to 'I' then H then E. By now Liza and Nigel had drifted back to Earth though Billy was still somewhere else. Liza and Nigel anxiously whispered, "Mind the..."

"What the bloody hell is going on here?"

"Aargh!"

"I want me Mam," screamed Billy. He jumped up so quickly that the desk was knocked over, the letters were spread across the floor and the glass bounced underneath Miss Pike's desk. We looked at Billy and then saw big bad Pam. Unable to talk with my heart in my mouth, I realised that the dinner lady could get us into even more shit.

"Pick that bloody mess up."

Billy ran to Pam and put his arms round her. "I want me Mam," he whimpered again.

"Don't be such a big baby. You should have known better, the lot of you. Whose idea was this?"

In true Black Team form we all looked at the floor and none of us said anything, though I went slightly redder than the rest.

"Well, why does that come as no surprise? I wonder indeed. Well, clear this mess up and then go outside for the rest of dinner-time. I won't tell anyone. There's no point now as it's near the end of term and you're being split up anyhow."

After we had cleared up, she sent us marching downstairs and outside. The other groups had congregated their own way in the playground and our team, as always, found the corner. We stood round each other, set fast in our thoughts. Towering Inferno broke the ice.

"Bloody hell, that was scary, eh?"

"Aye."

"Do you think we've got the ghosts in, then?"

"I don't know. We'll just have to wait and see."

There was a long pause. Nigel began to play football with something no-one could see and Billy had become fascinated by the lines on the playground.

"Still, at least we've got the rest of the week to be the one and only Black Team."

"And Monday's Sports Day so at least we'll have some fun then."

"Fun? Fun? How can you stand there and say 'fun', Liza? Running round a track, 100 metres, 200 metres, 400 metres, long jump, high jump and relay. I'm sorry Liza, but I wouldn't call that kind of self-induced physical torture 'fun'."

We would have to compete against the Blue, Yellow and Pink teams. The Pink Brigade were beginning to be nothing more than acquaintances now and I didn't feel particularly close to them anymore. Their behaviour towards the Black Team expelled any warmth that I might have felt for them out of school. When anyone in the Black Team stood up in class or attempted to answer a question there was always that feeling of someone ridiculing you from behind, secretly giggling.

On the day in question, Liza won the 100 metres and Nigel won the long jump, of course, while Billy and I had yet to be given our sentences. We didn't have to wait too long. Billy was told he was in the high jump, which he duly lost. It was while we were consoling him that my punishment came through, the order given that I was to undergo the 400 metres. Liza gulped, Nigel closed his eyes and Billy collapsed. My beloved team mates were a source of pure encouragement.

Running was not my strong point and neither did I enjoy it. The only form of exercise I did enjoy was swimming, though coming from a fisherman's family it was viewed more as a necessity, like breathing. We could all swim from an early age and when we lived in Ireland we used to swim in the Atlantic Ocean. Certain members of the family had used this necessity to win competitions, and Peter was our family's champion though I now knew he was not the only one. In due course Maggie was to show me how important swimming could be.

All of a sudden we were off and by the time I had done 75 metres I was already feeling faint and my fellow competitors were literally a hundred metres in front of me by the time we reached the half-way mark. At last I reached the finishing line. I had come fourth - out of four. I suppose you could say I came last but at least I had seen it through, at least I had succeeded. As I stumbled over the line I could vaguely hear my team mates yelling and shouting words of proud encouragement as my heart pounded out of my chest. However, at least this inferior mortal could stand. Apparently Carly, who had come third, had collapsed and could not stand up for her medal so really I came third.

The Black Team had to stay behind and clear things away.

"I'm knackered."

"Come on, short stuff."

"It's not fair."

"Come on, Becky, give us a hand with this." I looked at Liza and the crate of bean bags and skipping ropes. Billy and Towering Inferno were stacking the chairs. I picked up the crate.

"How could they do this to us?"

"We're the Black Team."

"This was supposed to be Fun Week. Fun for whom, that's what I'd like to know. I mean, not only do I get branded as a non-conformist and sent down to do another year with Miss Pike, now they try to kill me by making me run 400 metres in the summer sun."

"Well, you came third."

"I came last."

"You came third. Carly collapsed and couldn't stand up. At least you could." I looked at Liza and a smile came up from my stomach. Billy and Nigel came running in.

"Hey you two, let's go home."

"But we haven't finished."

"It doesn't matter, all the teachers have gone home. Besides, Uncle Jack's here now."

"But what will they say?"

"Hey, we're the Black Team! We can't be relied upon to do any-thing."

As we walked home past the haunted house, I saw Auntie Maggie standing at the window watching us. As we silently passed I waved to her.

"Do you want to go in and see Auntie Maggie?"

"No thanks, Becky, some other time, eh? I'm knackered."

"I'm more knackered than you."

"No, I'm much more knackered than you."

"I'm absolutely, terribly, petrifyingly knackered."

We were both too tired to argue any more.

"See you tomorrow, third from last."

Sports Day was one that we went to bed early and a day we never forgot, although the last few days of that term were very strange and never to be forgotten either. When we returned to school next day, Uncle Jack the caretaker approached us. We thought we were in for it because we'd left things in such a mess.

"You did a damn good job clearing all that sports stuff away."

We glanced at each other. We thought he was kidding. Billy looked at him.

"What, really?"

"Yeah! You kids did a real good job. I honestly thought I'd have to clear up after you but you proved me wrong. Thanks a lot. You really showed them." Uncle Jack strolled away and Liza turned to the three of us.

"What the hell was that all about? We left the place in one hell of a mess."

"Yeah!"

We were silent for a while until Nigel suddenly mumbled, "You don't think it was anything to with the ghosts, do you? I mean, we did give them the weekend to move in."

My team mates looked expectantly at me. But what could I say? I didn't really think it would work, it was just a bit of fun. But things started happening on those final days of term. Things would go missing. Pens and pencils that you had just put down would be gone when you went to pick them up again. Chairs and desks moved around as well. The lights flickered on and off, conveniently above the Black Team's table. The contents of packed lunches went missing and soda bottles exploded.

By the end of term everyone was thankful to get out of school, including Miss Pike. Though I suppose having the chair pulled away from you when you're about to sit on it and no-one nearby to blame is a bit off-putting. True to form, she still blamed the Black Team anyway but there was nothing she could do. She couldn't give us detention as that was Mr Lukas' job, though God had long since departed on 'an early holiday' and would not be returning. Nevertheless, those last couple of days it felt as if a huge weight had been lifted out of school, despite the little mysteries that occurred in our classroom...

—THIRTEEN—

It was not only in school that things were unhinged. Our house had become a battlefield. My father rarely showed his face anymore as he was constantly at sea, and when his ship did land he sometimes never bothered coming home, just stayed on the boat. On the odd occasion when he did appear, he and mother did nothing but argue. More often than not it was about his staying away for too long, but their words hid a deeper meaning...

I knew why they argued. I knew what they were actually saying to each other underneath the empty words of hostility. And Auntie Maggie sensed there was something wrong with her favourite niece one afternoon while we tidied her garden as best Megan, Liza and I could, just before we broke up for the summer holidays. An Amazonian mixture of rain and sun that spring had transformed Auntie Maggie's garden into a fierce jungle, with dandelions taking the place of sunflowers.

"What's wrong, niece?"

"Nothing."

"There must be something, dear?"

Liza carried on attacking the four-foot weeds while Megan began to swim in them, her arms lunging down into the sea of weeds as she pretended to blow water. Mrs Doherty was still so concerned for Megan that she made her wear gloves and a scarf in July, which made her look ridiculous while we just had shorts and tee-shirts on. At least she had forgone the woollen hat by May. If Mrs Doherty could, I believe she would have wrapped Megan in cotton wool. This was the first time she had been allowed to play since she came back from the hospital.

"Well, you're very quiet."

"Just thinking."

"Oh, thinking is very good for you but don't overdo it. You know, everything in moderation."

I gave a half-smile.

"I mean, you don't want to think too much, people go mad that way." And Auntie gave a little nod. Liza and Megan had now both begun to play in the weeds. She turned to them. "Come on, you two, you're supposed to be cutting them down not swimming in them." She turned back to the weeding, still saying under her breath, "Not swimming in them... not swimming in... not swimming in... not swimming..." I could see her getting more and more wound up with every word, every mention of swimming, as she began to hack at the ground with her trowel. There was only mud there but she still stabbed the ground, piercing it with the steel blade. I attempted to diffuse the situation.

"Auntie Maggie?"

Nothing.

"Auntie Maggie?"

Stab. Stab. Stab the earth. I put my hand on her shoulder.

"Auntie Maggie?"

She stopped and stood to attention.

"There's lots of weeds over there under the tree. Let's go and dig them out."

Auntie glanced across to the big oak tree. "Poor oak tree, it's being strangled by all those weeds." She gathered her garden tools and we went to the tree. She looked up. "Hello, niece."

"Hello, Auntie."

"What's wrong?"

"Oh, the usual." She waited for me to continue. She didn't know what I meant. "Parents." I shrugged.

"Oh."

Auntie began to pull the weeds up. "So many this year."

"Yes."

I sighed and stared down the street, up the walls of houses to rooftops and chimneys. I tried to imagine what it would be like to take flight away above the roofs and bricks to what lies beyond.

"Do you like to run, Auntie?"

"Run?"

"Yes, to stretch your legs and run. Feel the power and freedom of running. Just run."

"Run? Like water?"

"Run away?" Megan and Liza had swum their way over to us. Megan still blew bubbles and waved her arms about. "You mean run away from home?" said Liza.

"Aye, and see what's out there, over the houses and up above the trees."

"Th... there's a rainbow sssoaring in th... the sssky!" bellowed Megan. I smiled.

"Aye Megan, up where the rainbow lives. Run away and chase the rainbow."

"That would mean you'd have to leave your home."

"What's a home but a house, Auntie Maggie? Let's run away tonight!"

"What, all of us?"

"Everyone."

"Everyone ch... chase rainbow!"

"Aye, why not?"

"We'll need things for the journey. Food. I'll get some crisps, my

Mum's always got crisps in the cupboard for our pack-ups, and my brothers eat them by the dozen."

"I've got some apples."

"Fine. That's it then. We've got everything we need."

"When do we want to go?"

"Well, I don't think my Mum will let me run away during the day so it'll have to be at night."

"Rainbow g… go to b… bed at night!"

"Well, we can see it when it wakes up in the morning then."

"Yeah!"

"Aye, the night's the best time to run away. It's so full of magic."

Auntie Maggie raised her eyebrows at me. "Are you sure, niece?"

"Aye. Let's run away tonight."

"Where are we running to?"

"I don't know. Let's just see when we get there."

"Can I bring my teddy bears?"

"Not all of them, no."

"But who'll look after them when I've run away?" Liza was aghast. "No, my brothers'll knock the stuffing out of them."

The rest of that afternoon we pulled weeds together and generally made a path to Aunt Maggie's door. It didn't occur to us that if we were going to run away there would be no need to tidy the garden as there'd be no-one in the house to enjoy it. Each of us worked silently, no doubt thinking what it would actually mean to run away, to leave. I don't know what Megan thought of home, what it meant to her. Probably to her home was her Mammy, it was a person. But to me it was just a house and the people I longed to escape from. A family of arguments, lies and secrets that were never discussed even though everyone bloody knew them.

That night I wanted the darkness to come quickly and surround me. I grew impatient and stared out of my bedroom window, wishing and praying that night would smother the town with its presence. But it didn't come no matter how much I prayed for it. I sat on the bed waiting, watching the evening through my window, then laid down on my soft bed watching the light bounce from my bedroom ceiling. When I woke up, it was night, darkness surrounded me. My bed held me close but I wanted to run away this night. I pulled myself free of the bed, crept out of my room and into the empty darkness of the stairway.

The moon was full and the night seemed alive as I stepped out of the door. I stood motionless, silently staring at the moon in all its glory. Darkness breathed through me. I didn't turn to look at the house but moved slowly as if in a dream; but this was reality, I was really running away. I tiptoed down the road like a pixie prancing on a mushroom to the house of my Aunt Maggie. She was standing in the garden in a ray of translucent moonlight, wearing a nightdress. As I drifted closer, her face became clear yet there was a look on it I'd never seen before. It looked like her yet it was not, as if someone had taken her place. She caught me studying her but neither of us said a word. We tiptoed to Megan's house.

I never thought for one moment that Megan would want to run away or that her mother would let her out of the house at night. But as we came to her gate we could see something through the frosted glass of her front door. Then the door opened and into the night stepped Megan, complete with bed socks and a shawl, whispering, "F... F... Find rainbow now." She tiptoed down the path in an exaggerated fashion and joined us on the other side of the gate. All was well, now it was Liza's turn.

As we approached her house there was no movement behind her door and no-one stood in her garden. We looked around, then Megan took some mud from Liza's garden and threw it at the window of teddy bears. She knew what she was doing. She didn't wait for anyone to tell her but used her own judgment. In that instant, I realised that I had become my father - oh how much I had wanted to run away right at that moment, but I could never leave Megan and Maggie behind.

Liza appeared behind the teddy bears. She looked at us and then opened her bedroom window.

"C… Come on, let's f… find rainbow."

"No, I don't want to, Megan. I want to stay with my teddy bears."

"C… Come on, Liza!"

"No, you go on. I'll see you tomorrow."

"But we're running away. We'll have adventures."

"You can tell me about them later."

And that was it, that's all that needed to be said. Liza was happy where she was. She didn't need to have adventures. She was perfectly happy for someone else to have them. She was happy with just the story of an adventure. She had no purpose to run away, unlike us. She closed the window and disappeared from our sight.

Megan pulled her shawl up round her. The night was warm and the air smelled sweet with the aromas of gardens and flowers that had been watered. Night-scented stock and honeysuckle mixed with the calm and silence. My bare feet stepped lightly on the coldness of the pavement. As Aunt Maggie quickly stepped in and out of the moonbeams, Megan followed and it became a skip then a run. Suddenly we began to gallop through the streets. We had no idea where we were running to but we WERE running away.

Our fears and dreams glowed in the darkness as night whisked us away for an adventure of nothingness and an awakening of transparent reality. The whole world was empty. No cars drove past as we ran through the streets in bare feet with nightdresses flying through the air. I had run this path before but now Auntie was leading us.

The dock lights twinkled into view. We ran to the end of the jetty and suddenly stopped. The path was finished. We had come to the end. There was nowhere else for us to run to. Next stop was the sea.

We stood there at the end of the jetty staring out to sea, the expansive black deep of currents and mysteries.

We never said a word, each lost in our own thoughts. I had no idea what Aunt Maggie or Megan were wondering, but I thought of everything, the meaning of it all. Why I had wanted so desperately to run away. What it was I was running away from. Where I was going. And what had stopped me from continuing.

I had hated leaving Ireland but that was because it was all I had ever known. Ireland had been my world: my family, Aunt Siobvon and her arrogance, my father and his lies, mother and her secret stolen moments of pleasure. But here I was now with friends and an aunt I'd never known existed. As I gazed out upon the vast open darkness of the sea, I realised what home was. It was not a place, a house or a country but the people, the friends and family that I played with, talked to and knew. Home was what I knew in my heart and my heart was with Megan, Aunt Maggie and even Liza. I had no need to run away for I was home when I was with them.

As we returned to our houses, I walked in the middle with Auntie Maggie holding one hand and Megan the other. I felt I had been on a long journey and was now returning, and I smiled for it felt good to be home. Our adventure had lasted probably about half an hour but it had been worthwhile. We never shared with Liza what had happened. Well, nothing much had happened apart from the fact I now realised I never wanted to run away again. No matter how difficult things got at the house I lived in with my family, I could always go home to Megan and Aunt Maggie. That summer was the beginning of my revelation.

The summer holidays were once again upon us and little did I know how they would really affect me, how different everything would be when I eventually returned to school. A lot was to happen before then. The holidays were days of doing exactly what we wanted; no work, no school, just play all day. Towards the end of the first week, Megan, Liza and I were sitting outside doing nothing, just thinking about the marvellous holidays and what games we were to have.

"I'm bored," Liza muttered.

Megan nodded and I gave a little sigh.

"I'm really bored."

"I believe you."

"No, I'm serious, Becky. I'm dangerously bored."

Megan sighed and crossed her arms. Liza looked down the far end of the street and noticed Katie, Suki and Carly. They all looked the same as us, absolutely, completely, painfully bored. By the beginning of the second week we had begun to move towards one another and by the middle of the week we had started talking. It really is amazing what boredom can do to one.

I cannot exactly remember whose idea it was but I truly believe it was Megan's. She said it very softly and clearly.

"It hot. If only we c... cool d... down."

Remembering our Science lessons, Liza recalled that water cools one down. Suddenly she said, "How about a water fight?"

Our eyes lit up, we were children again. But holding out her pink dress, which had ribbons and lace bows on it, Suki uttered, "But when? I can't have a water fight in this. I'll ruin it."

Carly nodded. "That's right, Suki. And I don't want to ruin my gold sandals." She pointed to her feet and we all looked down at her gold sandals. Megan, Liza and I looked at each other in our scruffy tee-shirts and dirty old cut jeans. We turned back to our pretty blonde friends and said the only word we could.

"So?"

"So I'm going home to get changed. Simple as that," said Suki, and with that she stormed off home to get changed, followed by Carly.

Katie had said nothing the whole time; now she just looked at me and smiled, shrugged her shoulders then followed on after the others.

Liza looked at me and shrugged her shoulders. "Women!"

Megan and I nodded in agreement.

I really have no idea how, but the word got round that on Friday the twelfth of August there was going to be a water fight. So for the rest of the week children who lived in the avenue and surrounding area saved squeezy bottles and anything else they could lay their hands on for a weapon. It was while I was fighting with Peter that I realised my brother and sister knew.

"Hey, that's my squeezy bottle."

"No it isn't, little one, it's mine."

"No it bloody isn't, Peter. I've been waiting all week for this."

"So have I."

"What for?"

"For the water fight."

"How do you know?"

"Everybody knows."

I tightened my grip on the squeezy bottle. "Well, you're still not having it, you shit."

"Oh! Naughty, naughty. Daddy's little girl swearing. You just wait `til I tell Mammy."

"What's going on?" demanded Leah.

"She wants the squeezy bottle for the water fight."

"Honestly Peter, I'm surprised at you lowering yourself to fight with her over a bloody squeezy bottle. Let her have it, we'll devise other weapons to drown her with."

Peter let go. His grip was so strong that when he released it I fell to the floor. Towering above me he seethed, "You might as well have it. I'd only have thrashed you with it."

I held my squeezy bottle close and silently declared war. At last D-day arrived I raced round to Liza's house with my giant bottle firmly clenched in my hand. Just as I reached up to the doorbell, the door opened; it was her mother.

"Hello, Becky. Well, come on in, love. Liza's just finishing her tea."

I followed her through to the dining room and sat down. Liza saw my bottle.

"Cor, that's a big one. Look at the size of that, Dad."

"Aye. You'll be able to do some damage with that, young Doen."

"You know about the water fight, then?"

"Of course. You should've been here yesterday tea-time when the squeezy bottle finally ran out. What a commotion. Of course, Liza got it in the end."

I glanced around and wondered where Liza's brothers were. She noticed me looking. "They've all gone to their mates to get ready and gang up on me." I smiled at the thought of Liza's brothers ever ganging up on her. It was ridiculous.

Mrs Edwards came back in carrying a plate of sandwiches and handed them to me. "Here you are, Miss Becky Doen. Hope you enjoy them. Every kid we know loves those sandwiches."

I took a bite and salad cream trickled down my chin. "Salad cream?" "Aye. Aren't they just the business?"

"Aye. But I've never had them before."

"Never before?"

I was amazed to find another adult who knew what children liked. I had Mrs Doherty with her creamy bar cola and now I had Mrs Edwards with her salad cream sandwiches, not forgetting the tomato ketchup ones she had made before. What more could any child possibly want?

After Liza had finished her tea we waited in the avenue for war to begin. The parents must have known something was going on as every child that Friday was as good as gold, helping their parents without moaning, setting tables and washing dishes without a word.

They did everything to ensure their parents left the house early. Then we filled our squeezy bottles, water pistols, buckets, balloons and anything else that could be used as a weapon. I think there was a water shortage that week.

Megan's mother had gone out and left Megan in the care of her Aunt Sophie, a rather senile and elderly lady who could neither see you nor hear you unless it was something she wanted to see or hear. Aunt Sophie chose not to hear Megan creeping out the house when the rest of the avenue did, so we took it as if she had given us her blessing.

Twenty-five children stood in the avenue, all of different ages, different shapes and sizes, with no adults telling us what not to do. We stood so quietly that the avenue was even more silent than when we were inside our houses. Everyone glanced at one another wondering who would be the one to make the first move. There were no teams here, no sides, it was simply everyone for themselves. We had come well equipped; buckets of water were at our sides while our hands eagerly toyed with our weapons. Suki and Carly had got little pink water pistols that looked puny next to my jumbo squeezy bottle.

We waited anxiously for the beginning, for that first move. Listening to the silence, I had no idea that my brother and his friends were standing right behind me. All of a sudden... WHAM! A balloon filled with cold water slammed onto my head, stunning me for a moment. I turned round to see Peter's smiling face. I picked up a water balloon and played with it in my hands, but just as I threw it he ducked and one of his friends standing behind him got it right in the face. He threw one back but it hit one of Leah's friends in the face. Thus it began.

The avenue burst into life, filled with twenty five screaming, shouting, running, screeching children throwing water over anything that moved. It was mass hysteria; friends turned into enemies and enemies turned into friends. I really did enjoy pelting Suki - it was something about the way she screamed that brought the devil out in me, plus it made Megan laugh.

This water fight was one of the very few moments in my childhood that I was happy to have Peter and Leah with me. They behaved like a brother and sister to me; when someone pelted me they would bombard them right back. Then they would thrash me. The water fight made enemies but it also made friends I would never have dreamed of. It's strange what war can do. Yet some friends were not true.

In the days and weeks that followed, Suki and the others began to call for Megan at her house just as Liza and I always had. With our new-found friends we now played for hours up and down the avenue.

Mrs Doherty had grown to accept me but she could not accept the Pink Brigade. She put up with them for the sake of her daughter but she knew that this new-found friendship would not last long. One day she came out of her house to check on Megan, saw us then straightened up and stood to attention with her arms crossed.

"You know, it really is amazing."

Liza looked up.

"What is, Mrs Doherty?" Suki ventured.

"Well, to see you all playing so nicely together. It's hard to imagine that not so long ago you called my daughter names. And this time last summer you made her smell a dandelion when everyone knows that if you smell a dandelion you wet the bed."

We looked at Megan who smiled, oblivious. As for Katie, she looked surprisingly guilty.

"Sorry, Mrs Doherty."

Suki gave Katie a sharp look. She wasn't sorry even now that she had got to know Megan and was also playing with her. At that moment, I wanted to get up and walk away; Suki didn't get it, she just didn't understand.

"Well, I'm glad you're sorry. And I'm glad to see you playing together." Mrs Doherty uncrossed her arms and was about to go back inside when she looked again straight at Suki. "I hope for your sake you don't turn back to your old ways, because if I catch any of you being spiteful to my daughter then you'll certainly know about it from me." She turned round and marched back in.

I glared at Suki. "You did that? You made Megan smell a dandelion?"

Suki smiled. "Sure did."

"How could you?"

She didn't answer. I said no more but let out a deep sigh and turned away.

—FOURTEEN—

When we passed Auntie's house I would often see her peeking out of the window watching me. But the Pink Brigade were still frightened by the house. Suki would see me looking up at the windows and she in turn would look up; occasionally she would see something but was so frightened that she quickly turned away. Yet they were still enthralled by it and on days when we were too tired to run and play we would all sit on the pavement and listen to Suki creating her stories about 'the witch'.

"Well, she's hunched over like this. She's got a long nose with a big wart on it and her skin's green and she walks like this…" Suki would burst into drama and begin to 'walk like the witch'. Then Carly began to copy her and Megan started laughing, which encouraged Katie to stand up and do 'the witch's way'. Apart from having green skin and a wart at the end of her nose, apparently the witch fed on humans, especially children. Little girls were her favourite and a delicacy while little boys were common and not that tasty. When the witch wanted to go anywhere she used her broomstick, which had wings on it so she could go extra fast. She also had a baby dragon that she locked outside in the rain to stop him from burning everything when he yawned.

Megan seemed enthralled by all this fiction. I think she had no idea who exactly they were talking about, just thought it was a fairy story. After all, we knew the house was not haunted - just lived in. So we sat round listening to them as they contrived and fabricated, formulated and revised the story of the haunted house until it matured into a bright flame of invention for Liza.

"Why don't we put on a play about the wicked witch?"

The Pink Brigade thought this a great idea and decided to make some costumes. As she was the smallest, Carly became the pet dragon. Suki, who always thought of herself as a good saint, would be the priest who, instead of wearing the normal black, dressed in white. Actually, it was an old sheet of Mrs Doherty's with a head cut out so she wouldn't look like a ghost. Katie was to be the black cat, with black gloves and an old black jumper and a long black scarf of Megan's which we tied round her waist for a tail.

And who, you might ask, would be the star of the show? That part went to Megan who made an excellent witch and had got the walk down to a fine art after Suki had shown her over and over again. We had no green make-up but Megan found a green witch's Hallowe'en mask in her play trunk. Liza and I were the children she ate - I was the boy because I had short hair and Liza was the girl because she had long hair. Obviously.

The summer streets sparkled with our imagination, though we were filthy by the end of the day. Our faces and hands seemed to have picked up every speck of dirt and dust that was floating in the atmosphere. Megan went in early on the nights she had to go to church because she had to have a bath. It was simply 'not on' that she could go to church 'looking like a road sweeper'. But after Megan had gone the play didn't feel the same and we just sat around not wanting to carry on without her. It was as if she made it. The part simply belonged to Megan. She was the star of the show. So we sat in the sun's evaporating rays and watched the shadows grow longer.

When Megan came out of her house, she dawdled at her gate. We smiled and she rocked from side to side. Her dress was a pale apple green with a mixture of buttons and bows, her hair was in two plaits and the sun had brought out her freckles. Her mother came out in a flowered, short-sleeved dress and clean, crisp white cotton gloves.

"Come along, Megan, we don't want to be late for church."

Megan's hand automatically found her mother's. Mrs Doherty looked at the five dirty-faced hoodlums staring up at her from the gutter and smiled down at us. "Don't stay out too late, you dirty little buggers." We watched them march out of sight. Megan going to church was a regular event. For us it was a miracle.

"I wonder why they go to church."

"To pray." Katie shrugged.

"They say the devil lives under the church," said Liza.

"Who says?"

"People."

"Why?"

"Because it's a good place to hide? Right under your enemy's nose."

"Yeah, but why go to church to pray?"

"Well, maybe the believers won't have to pray so hard when they're dead." I don't know why I said it. The words just seemed to come out of my mouth on their own, but the moment they escaped I regretted them. The others all turned to me and no-one spoke for ages.

The long hot summer days were spent acting out the so-called true story of the haunted house. We elaborated it more and now, instead of just sitting in the witch's den, the dragon would fly to the priest's house and spy on him to find out what he was up to, then fly back to the witch to report what he had seen. Megan was marvellous when it came to her big scene. She would turn round and round so much that she made me feel dizzy just watching her, then she would suddenly stop and fall down. The witch was dead. The end.

Play rehearsals continued into the evenings. We never knew what we were rehearsing for. Little did we know how much the end of the play would affect the actors, especially two members of the production.

Ever since the running away escapade I had grown closer than ever to Aunt Maggie and especially to Megan. I began to have nightmares that something was coming to take her away. I'd lie awake in my bed listening to the sounds of our house murmuring and creaking at night. It had been so easy to run away that night that I knew I could leave the house again without mother hearing me. And some nights I felt compelled to go 'home' - I would creep out of the house and run down the street to Megan's house, just to sleep on her doorstep. I don't think anyone ever knew apart from Aunt Maggie; once or twice I saw her looking at me through the curtains but she never said anything. It was something I had to do. Then as it began to get light I would creep back into my own house.

That summer was the hottest we had ever known and it even went into the record books. At times it was too hot for the haunted house play and instead we hovered around in shade of the trees that loomed over the pavement. It was while we were loitering there one day that Liza uttered the obvious.

"My throat's dry. I could do with something fruity going down it."

We all murmured in agreement.

"Yes, but it's too far to walk home for a drink and besides I can't be bothered," sighed Carly. We gazed down the street.

"The shops are closer."

"Yeah, but I don't have any money."

"I've got some," said Suki. She pensively drew out of her pocket a fifty pence piece. It sparkled with images of fizzy cola bottles, strawberry laces, spaceships, jelly babies, space dust and golden nuggets. As we walked along to the shop that sold everything under the sun, we debated what would be the best, gooiest, non-nutritional, fruity substance we could buy.

"It has to be something that lasts."

"Something we don't have to eat all in one go."

"Something that's got different flavours."

Then we spotted it, a jar of beautiful, jaw-aching gobstoppers and at only five pence each. By the time we had got back to our trees the shade now dominated the entire pavement right past the kerb. We sat with our feet in the gutter and shoved the gobstoppers into our mouths. They were so big our cheeks filled out with them. They were all different colours and with the different colours came different flavours. We opened our mouths and showed one another what flavours we had. By the time we had got them down to half-size our jaws ached so much we had to take them out and wrap them back up in their paper.

The summer evenings eventually turned into shorter autumn evenings. The holidays were coming to an end and soon we'd be going back to school. Our play rehearsals were scrapped as friends had to going shopping with their mothers. Of course, my mother never took me although she did take Peter and Leah to get what they needed. It was always a last minute rush with me and I wondered if my father would be taking me this year. He had been away for some time but surprisingly I was glad to hear that he was now on his way back; I had missed my father. I decided to surprise him by meeting him when his boat came in tomorrow

The night was still far off but I could hear the deep bellow of a fog horn or a ship's horn somewhere out in the estuary, waiting to come in to the safety of the docks. The more I listened, the more I realised that I had never listened properly to the sounds of this town. It was a prosperous fishing port yet I had never really heard the ships' horns. For the very first time I was scared, scared for my father. I was a fisherman's daughter but I had no real idea of what life was like out at sea. I had heard the tales and I had been out on ships many times, but never really left the coast. I had never been in a trawler on the wild openness with nothing for miles around except the sea.

The horn sounded so frantic against the still calm of the late afternoon. It shouted out to anyone who would listen. I wondered how many people were listening and how many had switched off, oblivious to the horn as I had been since I arrived here nearly a year ago.

A storm was brewing. There was no sun. There was no rain. The ending was beginning. An empty shadow was preparing to leave the womb, ready to travel from the dark into the light. There were no white clouds. There was no blue, just a dead grey sky.

Megan and I were safe inside the nursery, playing with our dolls. I loved our silent moments together, just the two of us in our separate silent worlds, though soon our worlds would become one. Liza had recently gone on holiday with her parents. Suki and Katie had gone shopping together with Suki's mother. Carly had gone to visit her grandparents. Suddenly the clock struck five. My father's boat was due in soon.

I looked at Megan. "I have to go, Megan. I'm gonna meet my father."

"Wh... Wh... Where?" She had obviously forgotten that father was a fisherman. I had told her many times but each time she forgot. I suppose she thought it wasn't that important.

"At the docks. I'll be waiting for him at the harbour."

She nodded and finished dressing her doll. "Can I c... c... come?"

"Sure you can but would your mother let you?"

She shrugged her shoulders. "Ha... rrr... bour's not far!"

"You know the harbour?"

"Went t... to it with s... s... school!"

"Oh, right ye'are then, but we'll still ask your mother if she'll let you go."

Megan nodded obediently and went to the kitchen where, of course, Mrs Doherty was making a chocolate sponge for later on. When she saw Megan and me hovering at the door, she assumed we had come to see if the cake was ready.

"I haven't made the sponge mixture yet, you two."

I looked on while Megan answered, "No, it n... not for c... cake."

"Oh well, what's the matter then?"

"C... Can I go with Bekkeeee t... to m... meet her f... f... fatherrr?"

Mrs Doherty stopped measuring the sugar and butter. She turned straight to me and wiped her hands then smoothed down her apron. "When is your father due in, Rebekah?"

"Evening tide, Mrs Doherty."

Mrs Doherty looked at the clock and then at Megan, who seemed fascinated by a light switch. "That'll be soon. You'd better get moving, then."

On hearing this, Megan ran to her mother and gave her a big bear hug. Mrs Doherty shouted after us, "Better take a jumper both, it'll be cold on the docks and the fog's coming down thick and fast. Wouldn't be surprised if there's a storm brewing."

We raced out of the house so happy to be out together, just the two of us. As we skipped past Auntie's house I saw Maggie staring out of a window at me as usual. I wondered if she knew about the games we had played and realised who the play was about. I figured she did. I just sensed she knew and somehow that she was pleased with it. We both waved as we passed by.

The huge dock tower loomed closer and closer. We skipped silently until we reached the docks, alive with hustle, bustle and confusion. People were running to and fro. Bikes were falling over. The cars honked their horns for a lorry to move out of the way. The fish merchants lined the quayside eagerly awaiting their silver income.

Megan and I walked closer to the jetty. Huge thick ropes were laid upon the ground and we had to be careful where we trod for fear of tripping over them. We stood looking out to sea, our eyes firmly fixed upon the incoming trawlers. Then suddenly the Rachel Marie came into sight. We waved and watched as she slowly came into dock. When she landed, I ran to my father and Megan followed. I quickly glanced where I was going. Megan did not. We were right at the edge of the jetty and sixty feet of brown water that had trawlers chomping through it.

As I ran to father I had no idea what had happened until I saw the look on his face completely change from happy to sheer terror. I turned to see Megan disappearing over the jetty, then heard a splash.

I ran to the end of the jetty and, without thinking, jumped in after her.

As soon I hit the water, the first thing I felt was the coldness of the sea. It had had the sun beaming down on it all summer but it was still not warm. The next thing I felt was something pulling me. I thought it was Megan so I dived down to see if I could find her. My eyes were sore and couldn't see anything in this brown liquid, but something was pulling me down further and now I couldn't fight it.

The sweat and blood of men's lives fled into my lungs, killing my screams for help. Darkness surrounded me, brooding silently, waiting for the chance to take another life. Dreams and reality rushed by in one sweeping wave. I fell deeper and deeper into the silent world of death with no hope of seeing a glimpse of that light above, shrinking smaller. Suddenly I heard a splash. Someone broke into the silent world of the living, breathing she-devil sea. I felt a strong hand around me but before I could tell who it was I fell into sudden blackness.

No sound.

No light.

No touch.

No smell.

Nothing.

Just complete blackness.

—FIFTEEN—

ot, sticky pain all over my body in every single part. I have no idea where the pain is coming from. Hot and wet. I'm still wet. I'm still in the sea. Why am I in the sea? Megan. "MEGAN?"

"Shhh now, it's alright, Rebekah. It's over."

What's over? Where am I? What am I doing? What's going on? "What's going on?"

"Nothing, Rebekah. It's alright. Just relax and try to sleep."

For the next two and a half days this is what I felt. I was completely disorientated. I had no idea where I was or even who I was. In between slipping in and out of the darkness, I heard snippets of what people around me were saying. I distinguished two voices, mother and father, and I later found out that the other voice was the doctor's. I dreaded opening my eyes as they burned and stung me and water poured from them so I kept them tightly shut. I just listened to the voices around me. I could barely speak. My strength and voice were still at the bottom of the sea.

"What's happening?"

"Shhh, Becky. Please try and get some rest, dear."

A soft voice came tenderly to my ears, surrounding and cushioning me upon a cloud of feathers. To what angel did the voice belong? I tried to open my eyes but my tears solidified.

"Amy, I just can't risk it."

"But you said yourself she should be in hospital."

"Yes that's right, but she could die getting there."

"But isn't it worth the risk?"

"Yes, and if she went in an ambulance it would be safer as they have all the necessary equipment to deal with an emergency."

"Look you two, for the last time I am not moving Rebekah to a hospital. I just don't want to take that chance."

"But you said she could die?"

"I know, it's fifty-fifty. Either way she could die."

"Oh my God. Becky…"

A warm, soft hand held mine tightly but before I could acknowledge the soothing touch I fell again into the black hole of nothingness. I was hot one minute, cold the next. I tossed and turned. My head felt like it would split open. The pain went all through my body. Throbbing limbs were connected to fingers and toes that stung. The sharp pains struck my spine and with every spasm the clamminess and humidity would surround me, making it difficult to breathe. Then suddenly, within the blackness, I fell.

It was as if something were pushing me down and down, further and further down a deep, black hole. I was not gently floating, but connected to something that was pulling me strongly. I accelerated down into blackness that surrounded me all over, like I was en-tombed by the darkness.

I was not afraid. Though I was on my own going down into this darkness, I felt I was not alone. I felt someone or something near me, but I didn't fear it. I welcomed it. I told myself to open my eyes and, though I didn't expect to see my bedroom or the people around me, I was amazed at what I did see.

Still surrounded by blackness, in the far distance I saw a light of many different colours. I was fascinated by it. I longed to see better this ball of different colours that flickered and danced before my eyes. My thoughts were of nothing and no-one but simply of the light, for the light. The light danced then I became the dance and before I knew it I was in a field of yellow with a rainbow overhead. I had never seen a rainbow like this one. It was so close to me that I felt I could reach up and touch it. All around me were colours so clear and crisp, vibrant and new. The fresh blue of the sky danced in harmony with the warmth of yellow flowers that gently swayed without any breeze. A sweet scent rushed into my nose while overhead the brilliant rainbow colours gently cascaded down.

I began to look over the horizon. Apart from softly rounded hills there was a valley with a stream running through it. Near the stream I could see a young girl playing. She had red hair and wore it in two big bunches. I began to walk towards her but with every step forward I took two steps back. I tried everything to get her attention, but everything I did turned out the complete opposite to what I expected. I tried to shout but no sound came from my mouth. I tried to jump up and down and wave my hands but instead I sat down and my hands stayed by my side.

This place, to say the least, was very peculiar. I thought about sitting down and immediately found myself standing up. I didn't care about anything except reaching the little girl playing by the stream, but I was on one side and she was on the other. I was in the meadow and she was in the valley and I longed to be on the other side with her. I looked round and marvelled at this peculiar place that I felt a part of. The rainbow glistened above my head. The sky was birdless but filled with hundreds of tiny, shimmering silver stars.

I looked once more towards the little girl by the stream; she had stood up now and I could see she was wearing a green dress. Suddenly over the hill there appeared a group of children, all in white flowing dresses. Over their heads were pearly pink clouds that seemed to be hovering, and I had the distinct impression they were guarding the children. They glided towards the little girl. She had been playing attentively as if waiting for them. Then they took her hand and she went with them without hesitation. All the time the clouds hovered above until they reached the top of the hill. Then the clouds slowly rose higher and higher until they came to a big golden door that I took to be the sun, though it didn't burn my eyes to look at it.

I felt so utterly sad. The other children did not want me, did not want to play with me. They had not come for me, but I was sure they knew that I was standing alone in the meadow of yellow sunflowers. As they reached the top of the hill, the little girl who had been playing alone by the stream turned back and looked straight at me. She knew I had been there the whole time but she had left me feeling alone.

I looked straight into her face and, even though she was far away, I could see all too clearly as if she had been standing next to me the entire time. In her eyes I saw my own reflection: a child mirrored in a child's eyes. As I looked, I felt a burst of emotion as though I were seeing the end of an era. I was bidding farewell to a friend, a communion of childhood that would soon become a mere remembrance, flashes of rekindled pictures in the mind of a past well hidden in adult life, yet never completely forgotten. Then she slowly turned her head away and drifted out of sight to the other side, to where I could not see and where I did not belong.

I suddenly felt cold. They did not want me. I was not allowed to go to the other side to be with my friend; to be with the child known as Rebekah. How strange, the tear that dried on my cheek. It is still tight when I blink. It is forever there on my cheek, crystallised, taut and sharp like the pain from whence it came.

I felt clammy, as though I could not breathe. I was choking. Then I saw a bright light looking into me. I coughed and spluttered and opened my eyes. I saw my bedroom with my father and my mother at the end of the bed while the doctor shone his light into my eyes.

"I tell you, Sean, that was close. She was gone for a couple of minutes. But thank God, she's back."

"Aye, thank the Lord."

I lay in bed thinking of that place I had been to, the multi-coloured place I had found within the black of nothingness, and wondered about the little girl I had seen. I felt that I knew her. Her sweet serenity implored me to go near her and I wanted to, but couldn't cross the stream. I tried to think who she was. I knew I had seen and played with her. I remembered her beautiful red hair that she wore in two big bunches and her green dress that gently swayed in the sweet air when she stood up to see the other children coming for her.

And I could not forget the other children. I couldn't make out their faces but I knew they were children and probably all girls, for they all wore little white dresses. They were decorated differently as some had frills on them, some had bows while others had soft, peach-coloured roses sewn onto the sleeves. I had wanted to go with them so much when they took the little girl and left me standing alone, feeling utterly dejected and desolate. I grieved to be with them. Though I never saw their faces, I felt I knew them and that every child knew them. It simply was not fair of them to leave me feeling like this, like I was different in some way.

Days followed and I tossed and turned the nights away. The days were spent sleeping and trying to dream that place back again. For the whole time I was recuperating, my parents never left my side. When my father was not there, my mother would be nursing me, never leaving me even for the night. She would sit in the chair at the end of my bed all night, watching me or reading. Occasionally I would hear Peter and Leah.

"How is she?" they would ask.

"She's asleep."

"Can't we come in?"

"No. I don't want you to wake her. She needs her sleep, Leah."

"Yeah, it's important for her to rest."

"Shall we go, then?"

"Yes, it would be better if you did. And try to be quiet."

"We will. If there's anything you want, Mammy, let us know."

"Aye, if there's anything she needs when she wakes up, let us know."

"Thank you, Leah. Thank you, Peter. I don't think I need anything as yet but I'll let you know if I do."

"Okay, we'll see you, then."

All this was done in whispers, so quiet that I only caught every other word. I lay silently in bed, listening to their concerned conversations. The rest of the time I lay thinking of the place where I had been and the friends I had seen there. Though I did not know them, I still regarded them as friends.

The doctor came to see me every day and gradually I got better, though I was still bedridden. I was not all that sure what had happened to me; all I could remember was the sea, the darkness and that place. I was weak and could only manage to get up to go to the bathroom, with my mother helping me there and back, although once or twice Leah offered to help.

I was constantly sick. There were days when I went with nothing to eat as I could not keep anything down. Nights were the worst, as I would vomit throughout most of it. It felt as if my stomach had been flipped over. It was constantly fluttering and there was always a bad taste in my mouth. I felt so shaky that my teeth would jitter back and forth and I would shake all over. My stomach would jump up and heave. I lay in dread and fear, afraid to be sick, wanting not to be sick again, and simply to have a peaceful night's sleep. The nights were so lonely and seemed to last for eternity.

I tried to think pleasant thoughts, reminiscing about the little girl. If I thought pleasant things then I would not be sick and my stomach would stop fluttering. If I thought about being sick then more often than not I would be, much to my mother's displeasure, getting up with me to change the bed and my night clothes. There was always a glass of water by my bed. She doctored and nursed me, she rushed here and there.

"I'll get you a hot water bottle," she uttered as she covered me with the new blankets. "Do you want a glass of warm milk?"

"No, thank you."

"Are you sure? It's no bother."

"Yes, I'm quite sure."

If anything, drinking warm milk seemed to make matters worse. I lay in bed feeling like jelly all over as I heard my mother tiptoe up the stairs. It was late and she didn't want to wake the rest of the household. She came into the room, the hot water bottle in one hand and a mug of warm milk in the other. I smiled to myself. She gave me the hot water bottle.

"Put that on your stomach, Becky." Then she placed the mug of warm milk softly down on the bedside cabinet, soothingly saying, "This'll do for later." I managed a smile though I was already half asleep. Then I felt her warm lips on my forehead but I was simply too tired to say goodnight. This would be the nights.

I'm not too sure whether forgetting what had happened was a good or bad thing, but my mother remembered. She would always remember. There were whole nights and days I could not recall, the snatched pieces of my life. The childhood moments vanished within the deep blackness of an illness I could never understand. Trapped in darkness is not a place for a child.

After a few weeks my mother decided I was getting better. I agreed with her and said she had better get some sleep herself. So I was kissed goodnight and told that if I needed anything I was just to yell for her and she would come running. The light was turned off and the darkness surrounded me again, although this time I did not drift away to a beautiful place. Instead I tried to stay awake and feel every sensation that tingled through my body until everything went black.

I woke up in the middle of the night. It was dark and everything was so silent that I could hear only the sound of my own breathing. I was frightened by the dark. Things seemed to be moving but I was too frightened, so I just lay still in bed daring not to move an inch while all the time I began to get hotter and hotter. There seemed to be someone in the room with me but I could not make out who they were. I was scared and wanted to yell out. I wanted to call my mother but I was too frightened. All the time I was getting hotter and hotter, sweating and melting. I could feel the sweat in between my fingers and on the palms of my hands. I had to do something. I had to move, it was either now or never. I jumped out of bed so quickly that I felt dizzy, but I fumbled for the light switch and at last found it.

Somehow it seemed not quite as hot with the light on as in the dark, where my head seemed to fill more quickly with images. Faces would appear to me out of the darkness when it encased me, and shadows that seemed to shape into horrific beings with arms that reached out for me. In the dark I could hear screaming.

And now in the light I could remember everything. Megan had not screamed, she had simply gone under the water. And I had seen Megan again on the other side of the stream.

It was Megan.

—SIXTEEN—

Gradually I got better and began to distinguish day from night as my sleeping pattern came back to normal. But I felt weird, there seemed to be a fuzziness in my head and I felt light-headed. Peter lent me his television to watch in bed. He brought it in one evening, struggling with it through the door.

"Here ye'are."

I looked up to see him place the television on the edge of my bed and look round for a table to put it on. "Haven't you got a table, Becky?"

I shook my head. "No. Leah took it when she moved into her new bedroom."

"Well, we'll have to make do with this chair." With that he pulled the chair to the end of my bed and placed the television on it. "There, can you see that alright?"

"Aye. It's fine."

"You sure now?"

"Aye, Peter, it's grand."

"Well, alright then. Do you want to watch anything?"

"Mmm, I don't know."

"There's that programme on now that you like."

"Oh sure, put that on then." Peter turned the television on and sat down beside me on the bed. I looked up at my big brother.

"Thanks, Peter."

"Sure, it's nut'in." He got up to go. "If there's anything you want now, be sure and give me a call."

"Aye, I will Peter."

"That's grand, then." He bent down and kissed my forehead.

I smiled then settled down to watch the television. The night was coming silently, darkness yawned outside and shadows crept into my bedroom. The flickering lights of the television made me feel sick. My stomach heaved. The numbness of my mind returned and I felt a tingling sensation go up and down my spine.

I closed my eyes and when I opened them again the room seemed to jump back into place. I looked at the television and the scene I was watching was the one I had just watched moments before - but where had I been? I hadn't moved, so how was it that I was watching this scene again? What had happened to me? It felt like I had gone in front of time then gone back to my original time. I had gone to the future and looked back on the past, but the past was really my present. I was frightened and disorientated. I didn't know where I was or who I was.

My heart beat faster and faster while all the time the television pictures still flickered in front of me. Dancing light was all around my bedroom. I felt faint. There was a buzzing in my ears and a weird smell rushed into my nose but it was unlike the smell I had known in that other place. I closed my eyes and then it was blank. When I finally came round it was morning and my mother and father were leaning over me. The doctor sat near me on the edge of the bed, holding my hand and smiling softly. My mother's hand was over her heart and father had his back to all of us, gazing out of the window with his hands in his pockets. The doctor waited for me to recollect where I was.

"You've been out for some time, Becky."

"I was asleep."

"Were you watching TV when you fell… em, asleep?"

"Yes."

"Mmm, and how do you feel now?"

I thought before I answered. "Weird."

He cocked his head to one side and scrunched up his eyes at me. "What exactly do you mean when you say 'weird'?"

"Like I'm not really here. Does that make sense? "

He patted my hand. "Of course it does. It makes perfect sense to me. Becky, when you get well enough I'm going to send you to the hospital for some tests, just to make sure I've got you right, okay?"

I nodded in agreement and my mother stood silently with her hand still on her heart, but father turned round. He had a nervous smile.

"What do you think it is, doctor?"

The doctor got up from my bed and let go of my hand. "I think, Sean, it's epilepsy."

"Oh. How long will it last?"

"Hard to say, Sean."

"Well, if you wanna give me a prescription I'll send Peter for it when he comes in."

"It's not that easy, Sean. Becky really needs to be going to the hospital for some tests so we can fully distinguish what type of epilepsy she has."

"What do you mean?"

"Well, grand mal or petit mal."

"Oh." This was the first word my mother had spoken. "What kind of tests will she be going to hospital for?"

"EEG and possibly a CAT scan."

"Are they painful?"

"No Amy, more uncomfortable than anything. Look you two, don't worry. We'll do everything we possibly can."

"Thank you, doctor."

"Yes, thank you, Doctor Daniels. Is there anything we can do in the meantime?"

"Well, just basically what you have been doing. But most importantly don't let her watch TV in the dark or expose her to any flashing lights. In the meantime, I'll write a letter to the hospital to arrange the dates of her tests."

My father showed Doctor Daniels out. I looked at my mother who still stood in the middle of the bedroom with her hand on her heart. She looked around and saw the television.

"Wasn't a very good idea of Peter's."

"It's alright, the doctor didn't say I couldn't watch it, just said I wasn't allowed to watch it in the dark with the pictures flickering."

My mother put her hands up to her face and the look of pure horror on it made me feel utterly terrible. Then she screamed with tears running down her cheeks and ran out of the room. I wondered what on Earth the matter with me was. What was epilepsy and was it so bad? Did my mother know something I did not? Was I going to die in a month or a couple of weeks' time?

I heard father's heavy footstep upon the stairs, sounding almost too weighty for the little stair to hold it. He came into my room but said nothing, then went back out and into their bedroom. He opened the door and I could hear my mother sobbing as he gently closed the door. I strained my ears to listen but couldn't hear much, just the muffled sounds of them talking, definitely about me. Once again I felt alone and dejected, though in that other place where I first felt like this I was happy to be there. It had been so beautiful. They talked for what seemed like hours so I fell asleep. I woke up with the light on and Leah standing over me with a tray of steaming food.

"What is it?"

"Beans on toast, your favourite. I made them especially for you."

"Oh, you've had your tea, then?"

"Aye, we all had it before Daddy went to sea."

"Daddy's gone on a trip?"

"Aye, well he hasn't been out since... your... you know? Since your accident and that's well over two months now."

"TWO MONTHS?!"

Leah backed away as if from a caged animal. She had guilt written all over her face as she cowered by the door. "Well, I'd better let you have your tea. I'll come up for the tray when you've finished." And with that she leaped out of the door.

By the time I got round to eating my beans on toast, it had grown cold. I was in complete shock. I had no idea that it had been so long. I still could not remember everything; all I knew was that I had fallen in the dock with Megan and I was not sure what had happened to her. All I did know was that the last time I had seen her was in that other place where I did not belong... So I decided that when Leah came up to collect my plate I would get her to tell me everything. I didn't have to wait long. I heard her light steps bounce up the stairs, but as they neared my bedroom they got heavier. She paused at my door. She knew what I was going to ask her. After some moments of deliberation, she advanced into my bedroom.

"Well, have you eaten all your dinner?"

"Sit down Leah, I want to talk to you."

She sat on the edge of my bed. "Becky, look, maybe you're not ready for this."

"Ready for what?"

She looked down, her chin resting on her chest. "The doctor warned Mammy and Daddy not to tell you."

"Tell me what?"

"They thought the shock would be too much for you to cope with. I mean, she was a good friend to you."

"Leah, just what the hell are you trying to tell me?"

"Oh Becky, you shouldn't hear this from me."

"Leah, you can feel sorry later but for the last time can you please tell me what happened?"

"Well... Megan tripped and fell into the dock and you jumped in after her."

"I jumped in?"

"Aye. Daddy said you tried to save her but the current was so strong that it pulled you down. Then Maggie jumped in and saved you." Leah moved towards me and held my hand. "Megan drowned, Becky. She drowned. Her body was washed up on the beach five miles away."

I felt nothing. I folded my arms and felt the blackness cover me once more. When I came to, Leah was patting my hand. "You were gone for a couple of minutes there."

"Yes. It's the epilepsy."

"I know."

"Oh. Do you know what it is?"

Leah smiled. "I've no bloody idea."

I smiled back though all the time my heart had ceased beating. I felt cold, so cold. Leah put her arms around me and I snuggled my head onto her breast.

"I'm sorry Becky, I've been so horrible to you."

"It's okay," I answered, but I was not really there. I had drifted to where memory was stored. I thought of Megan in her green dress and her red hair.

"I was jealous of you."

"Of me? Why?"

"Everybody likes you."

"They like you too. You're the prettiest, Leah."

"Am I?"

"Yeah."

"Well, I'm sorry Becky, you know, for everything."

But this time I no longer answered. I was long gone to the land of memories, to the place where I had first met Megan. I could not believe she was dead, gone forever. The days now all became like my memories that flashed here and there. They rippled down from my mind, memories full of Megan. She had been my true friend.

The day eventually came when I had to have the tests and I was bundled into a waiting taxi. I had not ventured out since that fateful day. My mother and father sat either side of me, silent. Father gazed out of the window, my mother gazed at me. As the taxi raced up the avenue, familiar haunts came back to me. I could not bear to look at Megan's house. As we passed Auntie Maggie's I searched the windows for someone but the sparkle had trickled away leaving the house empty of its enigma. A new secret was beginning.

I had never been to a hospital before and I was a little excited but at the same time unbelievably frightened. I think father was scared, his grey ashen face giving it away.

"I'll see where we have to go," he said softly to my mother, who simply gave a nod in return.

We were directed to the children's ward and from there to the waiting room. It was small and the walls were covered with colourful mice and ducks. In the corner was a box of toys but no-one played with them. The children sat on plastic chairs with their parents.

My eyes drifted round the faces of anguish, the bodies of pain. Some had no hair on their heads and I wondered why. In the corner sat a girl who looked like Suki yet she had short hair, cut even shorter than mine. She was dressed in her nightie and underneath her pink dressing gown I noticed, just peeking out of it, what looked like a hot water bottle. It was clear and there was some kind of yellow liquid in it. She covered her dressing gown over it as I stared at her, then she searched my eyes and I turned away. A nurse came and called my name so I got up and followed her; so did mother but father remained seated. He didn't move. I looked back at the room, at the bald heads of silent children, at the girl with the hot water bottle and pink dressing gown. I never knew there were so many sick children.

"Come along, Rebekah," smiled the tall, white nurse.

Everywhere seemed so white, brilliant white - the walls, the ceiling, the floor, the cubicle where I got changed. Mother came in with me but I pushed her out.

"I'll help you get changed."

"I don't want you to. I can do it myself."

"No, please let me help you, Rebekah."

"No, I don't want you to. I've been getting changed on my own since I was two." I snatched the white gown out of the nurse's hand and snapped the cubicle curtain shut. I took everything off and put the gown on. It felt hard. The floor was cold and bare and walking down the corridor I noticed a clean, crisp smell that turned my stomach. The nurse opened the door and I was led into a big room. I felt small. A chair dominated the room and I was told to sit in it; next to it was a table with cotton wool and other objects, and everything seemed sharp and dead. I felt empty and so alone.

The nurse began to dab my head with icy cotton wool. I looked at my mother in the corner, frozen to the floor. In front of me there was another room and in it sat people in white coats behind a wall of clear glass. I could see them and they could watch me. A tall lamp was brought out and then a hat of wires was fixed upon my head. The nurse went out, the room went dark and the lamp was switched on and off, on and off.

They tried to entice my illness out of its cave and make itself known to their machines, to lure it out of the dark of ignorance into the light of their knowledge. After they'd finished, I was allowed to get dressed and when I came back out into the room my father now sat next to my mother. There was a little chair next to the doctor's table which had on it a dish of little coloured sweets. I presumed the chair was mine. I presumed the sweets were mine.

In between the crunching of chocolate goodies, I heard bits of what the doctor was saying to father and mother. "Petit mal... Zarontin... Don't expect too much from her at school... She'll never do any good..." I finished off his plate of sweets.

"Rebekah, they were for the other children as well."

I turned and smiled at my mother. As we walked out of the door, my parents shook the doctor's hand. He went to pat me on the head but he never got the chance.

"Thank you for the sweets, they were really delicious. And I'm terribly sorry about the chair." I smiled at him and walked away. The doctor looked back to see the dish empty and the children's chair in pieces on the floor.

Doctor Daniels, at least, was different; he had had to prescribe my medication. At first it was tablets but I pleaded with him that I could not swallow tablets.

"You swallow sweets down whole, don't you?"

I told him that was different. In the end I won. I had to take medicine three times a day, a horrible thick sugary medicine that sent a shiver through one's teeth.

Now that I had ventured outside to go to hospital I figured it was only natural to be allowed to go out and see Liza. I had not seen my friend for nearly three months. I found it odd that she had not been round to see me, but everything was about to be made clear. The Saturday before school started again I decided to go round and see her. At first my mother would not let me and declared it was far too cold; it was, after all, the middle of November. I pleaded with her to let me go and used every possible trick in the book.

"It's not fair."

"No."

"It's round the corner."

"No."

"You'll have time to yourself."

"No."

After about an hour of skulking around the house, mother agreed but I had to dress up warm like it was sub-Arctic temperatures. A big woolly hat was dumped on my head as I was not allowed to get my head cold.

"So where's the polar bear?" Peter smiled as he shut the door after me.

"You don't have to go with me, Peter. I know where Liza lives."

"It's no problem, besides I was going out anyway."

"Was you?"

"Aye."

"Really?"

"Aye. I'm gonna go and see Tony."

"Oh. Any idea when Daddy will be back?"

"None whatsoever."

"Aye, typical."

"Don't worry, little one, you've got me."

I laughed.

"You've got Leah."

"And I've got Mammy."

"Aye, and Mammy's got them bloody books."

After I had been diagnosed, my mother had hunted every library and bookshop for every medical book on epilepsy. She became a right little authority on it, though Doctor Daniels warned her to put them away as they were not much use to someone without proper medical knowledge. She would read things into them that were not really there and claimed that Doctor Daniels was dangerous, especially when she thought he was wrong about my medication. She decided to change how many times I was to take it through the day. My father, on hearing this, `phoned Doctor

Daniels who immediately came round to talk to mother and after some delicate persuasion she finally agreed that I was taking the right amounts.

Peter left me at Liza's house and patted me on the back. I walked up the path and knocked on the door. I was sure she was in and I was desperate to see her. Liza was the only one I could talk to about the dream I'd had, the dream of that place. I was sure she would know what it meant. But I was not to have the chance.

The door was opened abruptly by Liza's mother. I smiled, knowing this was a friend's face. Her salad cream sandwiches had sealed our friendship.

"Hello, Mrs Edwards. How are you? Is Liza in?"

Mrs Edwards did not open the door very wide but stood half-way behind it with only her head peeping round. "Are you well enough to be out, Rebekah?"

"Yes, I'm taking medicine now for my dizzy spells."

"You're still taking the medicine? Mmm, well, you're really not that well then, are you, if you're still taking the medicine?"

"But I'm going back to school on Monday."

"Are you sure about that?"

"Yes."

"Well, how can you go back? You still haven't got over that epilepsy."

"Mrs Edwards, is Liza in please? I really would like to talk to her."

"Look Rebekah, I'm sorry but I can't let you in while you've still got epilepsy. I don't want you to give it to Liza."

"I don't think it's catching."

"I really am sorry Rebekah, but you'd better be off home now before you catch cold. You go home now and lie down, try and get rid of that nasty epilepsy. Goodbye."

Mrs Edwards slammed the door shut.

I looked down and walked silently away from the tightly shut door.

—SEVENTEEN—

Although I did see Liza at school the situation wasn't any better. If anything it was worse. I remembered how the past used to be and the memories just made me realise how worthless the present was. People who had never spoken to me before would now come up to me and teachers would whisper "Poor thing" as I walked past. Children would stare at me and strangers would smile, sympathy oozing from the corners of their mouths like spit escaping.

Everything had changed. New faces and new names now sat in my class, and even the Black Team had changed. Miss Pike had a whole new class to persecute. I figured I was doing her a favour. Her favourite victim was still there which must have been comforting. How reassuring for her to come to school in the morning and know that the Irish free spirit nuisance still thrived in your class.

Her first words to me were not of sympathy. I would never receive that from Miss Pike; she was someone who never changed her attitude towards anyone no matter what had happened, no matter what had been said. She was the same to me as the very first day I'd entered the school just over a year before. In some strange way it was relief, as I knew what to expect.

"Well, you've finally come back have you?" The words dripped from her thin pale lips. The second thing was, "There's your old seat in the Black Team. I don't suppose you'll learn anything this year either."

'Not with you teaching me,' I thought. How I longed to say it out loud.

I sat down and glanced around me; at least there were no Katies or Sukis this year but there was no Billy or Nigel either. When I looked at Liza, she sort of smiled nervously then turned away. I could sense she felt uncomfortable by the way she wriggled in her seat like a worm. I stared out of the window and thought how good it was to be back at school.

Life regained some kind of normality - well, for other people, I suppose. After all, they lived in normality even if they didn't know what it was. Not for me. My mother was being a mother for the first time. The weekends were particularly difficult as I had nowhere to escape to. After breakfast one Saturday morning she plopped a bundle of books onto the floor in front of me. I had been happy just sitting watching telly but this had to go for, after all, I could not be allowed to succumb to boredom.

"What are these?"

"Books."

"What for?"

"To read."

"Why?"

"I don't want you getting bored."

"Why?"

"You're not allowed to get bored."

"Why?"

"Because you have fits when you get bored. Besides, you have to do something with your time these winter months."

"Well, I can go out and play."

"No, it's too cold."

"So?"

"The cold is no good for you. It's dangerous, it can give you fits."

"I thought you said getting bored gave me fits."

"Don't argue with me."

"I'm not arguing with you. I'm just saying."

"So am I and you're not going out."

"I'll get dressed up real warm."

"No. Now go and read a book, occupy yourself. Make sure you're not bored."

"That'll be the day."

"Watch it."

"I'm not supposed to remember?"

I slammed the door behind me and stormed up to my room. Megan was gone. Liza was frightened of me and for that matter of herself. She didn't understand what had happened. But whereas her mind twisted and turned to try and make sense of everything, I just accepted it and went with it all. It was ridiculous to swim against the tide for I needed all my strength for living. Liza was frightened of where she had been. I was frightened of where I was going, but determined to survive.

As for my dear Auntie, she was again in a mental hospital. I longed to run up to her and put my arms round her. She was a link to Megan, Liza and good times. I just had my books and spiders to keep me company for the coming winter. Peter played games with me but would lose interest very suddenly when I began to win, mumbling to himself that he had let me. As for Leah, she would come home from school and tell me about a boy she had met and how she dreamed about him at night and even made a cushion in the shape of a heart with his name on. Then she would go on about clothes that made her hips look big or a skirt that made her look tall. She would put on a fashion show for me. But I was just so tired from school that I just wanted to have my tea and go to bed. I know my brother and sister were trying but they had so much enthusiasm for life that they left me behind.

One evening I sat in bed reading. Father was getting ready for a trip. I never saw my parents talk anymore; the gap between them had grown wider and the silence was even more unbearable than their battles. There came a knock at the door, an official knock, loud and firm. I came downstairs and found father talking with three men, two of whom I didn't recognise but the other was Doctor Daniels. When father saw me his words were harsh and abrupt.

"Becky, go back upstairs. This is not for you."

"On the contrary, Sean, I think it is. She is the only one who can tell us what happened."

Father was quick off the mark. "I know what happened. Maggie pushed them in."

"Now, Sean, that's just what you think."

"And why would I think that, John?"

"Because Margaret has been an embarrassment to you from the day you realised she was different." I guessed what they were talking about and Doctor Daniels was right. Father had been embarrassed since he was a child. He simply didn't understand differences. Aunt Maggie was just his big sister. I glanced round the room at the men, not knowing what they represented.

"What's going on?" I asked.

One of the men knelt down and looked straight at me, at my own level. "Can you tell us what happened, Rebekah? Did Margaret push you in?"

"No. No, she didn't. Megan fell in and I jumped in after her."

"Don't listen to her, John. She doesn't know what happened."

I searched my father's face. "Yes, I do know what happened."

My father's eyes were fixed on the man kneeling before me. "You can't pay any attention to her. You can't rely on her word. She's confused. She has epilepsy."

"I still know what happened."

The man looked at father, as they all did.

"She doesn't understand anymore. Her thoughts are very unreliable because of the epilepsy."

I glanced at Doctor Daniels who shook his head.

"It's not fair to say that, Sean. Rebekah was there, she knows. Sean, she hasn't lost her memory. Don't make Rebekah like your sister. She's not." Doctor Daniels then turned to me and spoke in such a soft voice that it was almost a whisper. "Did Maggie push you in?"

I answered calmly. "No, she jumped in to save me. Megan was already gone."

"That's rubbish, she pushed them in."

"So what are we going to do with Margaret? Is she going to stay in the institute?" The man who had not yet spoken suddenly got his say.

"Sean, that's terrible. Maggie's no harm to anyone."

"A child is dead and Rebekah is mentally - "

"Mentally what? Go on, Sean, say it." Doctor Daniels waited. I waited too but no words came, just silence. Doctor Daniels calmly continued. "Sean, Rebekah has epilepsy, that's all. She's perfectly normal and healthy, she just has epilepsy and with her medication it's controlled."

"Nevertheless, Margaret is to stay in that institute. She should never have come out of it."

"Why?"

"Because it's quite obvious that she's unstable. She's a menace to society. She's dangerous."

"Granted, Sean, her thoughts are unreliable and her mood swings are a little unpredictable. But keeping her in that institution for the rest of her life is a crime."

Father did not listen. He had finished. "That's all I have to say. That's all you need to hear." And he stared at the silent man who simply nodded. Then he opened the door and watched the men walk silently away. Doctor Daniels passed me and winked and I replied with a smile, though I had no idea why.

Father softly closed the door, his chin resting on his chest. He didn't look at me though I badly wanted him to. I wanted to shake him. My anger raged within me but the pain silenced it. He never once looked at me as he walked past into the kitchen.

I went back to my room. Some time later I heard raised voices, my mother and father at it again. Then I heard a light step bounce up the stairs, it was Peter doing his usual three-steps-at-a-time routine. He raced to his bedroom and quickly closed the door. Leah was not long behind but her step did not bounce. She opened the door quietly for fear of waking me.

"It's alright, Leah, I'm not asleep."

"No, I guess you wouldn't be with them going at it downstairs."

"What's it about this time?"

"Oh, the usual." She avoided the obvious answer and proceeded to get ready for bed.

I quietly turned on my side and mumbled, "Me?"

Leah placed her hand on my head and gently began to stroke my hair. "It's alright. They've got to argue about something, so why not you? It makes a change." And she half laughed.

I smiled. "I suppose."

The voices raged on into the night as Leah and I slept curled up in each other's arms. Nonetheless, our father obviously wanted us to know he had gone. The door slammed and shook the whole house. I awoke with a start.

"It's alright, he's gone." My big sister held me tighter.

"He didn't even say goodbye." I murmured, as I buried my face in Leah's arms.

Thus was my existence. Father hardly ever came home, so not much change there, but much to my displeasure my mother had now changed. She watched me like a hawk, waiting to devour me the minute I let down my guard. I actually preferred her before when she didn't want me around.

One day she caught me looking at the wallpaper. I wasn't allowed outside because it was cold so I couldn't make shapes out of clouds, so I made faces and shapes from the pattern of the wallpaper instead. But mother decided it was too dangerous for me to execute my imagination and attempted to put a stop to it.

"What are you staring at?"

"Nothing."

"You're having a fit, aren't you?"

"No."

"Yes, you are."

"No, I'm not."

"Stop staring."

"I'm not staring. I'm looking at the wallpaper."

"You're staring at the wallpaper."

"No, I'm not. I'm just looking at the patterns, they make great shapes."

"Well, stop staring at them."

"Well, stop staring at me."

"I'm not staring, I have to watch you every minute of the day."

"Why?"

"To stop you from having a fit."

"I don't have fits."

"Yes you do."

"No I don't."

"Yes you do."

"No, I have dizzy spells."

"Those are *fits* and they're caused by you staring."

"There are faces in the wallpaper."

"Oh, my God! I'm calling the doctor. Now you're imagining things."

"SHIT!"

"Don't you dare say that to me!"

"Why not?"

"Because I'm your mother."

"I'm surprised you remembered."

"You little bitch! Where are you going now?"

"OUT!"

"No you're not, it's damp outside and the air will make you have a fit."

"I thought that was just the wallpaper."

I stormed out of the door before she had time to answer and breathed in the fresh air and the relief of getting away from her. Across the road, Auntie's house looked more derelict than I thought possible. I walked passed Megan's house; it looked so cold and dead compared to the other houses. Weeds had grown up amongst the flowers and stuck in the middle of the garden was a For Sale sign. I closed my eyes and when I opened them Leah was standing beside me with a coat.

"Mammy says it's getting damp and you should put your coat on."

"She's driving me crazy, Leah."

"I know she's a bit much. But she cares."

"I'd never have known it a year ago."

"Things change, Becky. People change."

"But why?"

"Well, we have to and… and things can't stay the same."

"But why? Why did this have to happen?" I nodded to the For Sale sign in the garden of a house that was now dead. Leah bent down to fasten my coat, her voice soft.

"I don't know, Becky. I wish things would always stay the same. But they just can't and life goes on."

"And life ends."

Leah's eyes showed that she had no idea what to say. My poor sister didn't know whether to cry or ignore what I had said. She stood up straight, my coat now fastened, and smiled. "Let's go for walk, eh? Maybe mother will have something else to do by the time we get back."

She had chosen to accept it but at the same time ignore it. I understood, I knew there weren't any answers. I put my hand in my sister's and we walked as far as the park. It was a cold day, a day which wasn't yet sure whether it wanted to be autumn or winter. We walked silently and I breathed in the cascading colour.

Leah was right, things have to change just like the seasons. She realised that change was necessary but at times like these, the moments we spent together just silently drifting through the park, I sensed she did not want them to end either. Especially when we came to the bandstand.

There was a gang of boys Peter's age sitting on the edge. Leah preened herself. Her face went red and a flustered expression came to her face.

"Do you want to fart, Leah?"

"No. Be quiet. There he is."

"Who?"

"Mark."

A gangly youth with dirty blond hair that dripped into his eyes had his legs sprawled over the bandstand walls.

"Hello, Leah," he said in a really deep voice that didn't seem to come from him.

"Oh, hi. I didn't see you there."

"But - ouch!" A quick thump hit my ribs.

Leah seemed to tiptoe over to Mark. Her eyelashes fluttered and she gave out intermittent fits of laughter, full of frothy giggles, at every other word he said. He walked with us through the park though I never really noticed him. Now, Leah didn't want anything to change.

But the night closed in quickly. By the time we arrived home, the fog had slowly crept over the town that was preparing itself for another winter. The fog horn had guided us home with its cry. That night was dark and damp, the fog hanging from the street lights. Leah and I lay in our beds listening to the mechanical owl screech out through the darkness to fishermen far out to sea, calling them, guiding them like a siren back to a town surrounded by jagged rocks of fear.

I heard Leah quietly ask, "Do you think Daddy's safe?"

I pulled the blankets around me and turned to the wall. "Unfortunately, yes."

In time both Leah and Peter would spend more hours with their friends than with me, and I would miss them too.

As for Aunt Maggie, she was put into yet another institution, thanks to father. Some people said she was unable to cope with the outside world; I would wonder how many of us can. Father never went to see her, but in the years that followed I went many times to visit her. I brought her trophies and medals, to put in her room. I don't think she ever really knew who I was though; I had grown up a lot since that little girl she had first seen, when Liza and Megan had introduced the auntie I'd never known I had.

She did, however, talk about a little girl with red hair who wore it in two big bunches and who liked green ribbons, clouds and rainbows.

—EIGHTEEN—

I went to school for the best part of three days at a time because I simply could not get up early enough, having spent the entire night awake and vomiting. However, Miss Pike did not approve of all the time I had off school. It was easy to see what she thought of sick children, as a couple of times she sent the Education Welfare Officer round to our house. Unfortunately for him, he ran into father instead who told him in a polite, fisherman's sort of way, where to go.

But when the new Headmistress, Mrs Temple, found out, she was angry to say the least. Miss Pike received a sharp rebuke and Mrs Temple called my parents in to her office to apologise as she had no idea that Miss Pike had overruled her authority until the education officer returned to school to report. The education officer, by the way, was Miss Pike's brother, needless to say.

It was during the conversation between Mrs Temple and my parents that it was established that I should not let my mind wander and I was not to be allowed to become bored for one minute. Thus, in free time or storytelling I had music lessons with Mrs Temple, who graciously taught me the guitar. I especially didn't mind missing Miss Pike's storytelling; it was to say the least dull as hell, a bit like her.

Mrs Temple was indeed my salvation. She had swept into the school like the light of dancing colours that had swept into my life.

She wore bright green tights, a purple woollen dress, a brilliant orange cloak folded over her shoulder and she had a head of cropped, snow-white hair. She was simply my subconscious made real. I had lost Mrs Doherty and Mrs Edwards, but Mrs Temple was really all I needed and what's more she was the Headmistress. While Mrs Doherty and Mrs Edwards had brought creamy bar cola and salad cream sandwiches, Mrs Temple brought cheese; her hands or mouth were always full with a cheese of some kind.

And she was basically all I had, as Liza had become a master at avoiding me even though we were both in the same class. My fellow Black Teamsters were simply acquaintances, but I had to talk to Liza. There was something I had to say and I knew she was the only one who would understand.

One afternoon at Break I saw her in the corner of the playground standing by herself. As I walked nearer I could see her face change; she was thinking how to get away from me. "Stop squirming, Liza."

"I'm sorry, Becky." She looked to the floor, her body slightly twisted away from me.

"Liza, you're not gonna die. I haven't got the plague."

"Are you sure?"

"Yeah, bloody sure."

Liza glanced up and smiled, then there followed a long pause that seemed to last an eternity. Both of us had questions that would carry through the rest of our lives. She looked up, our eyes met and we could see what the other was thinking. No names were needed, only memories and tears.

"I don't believe she felt a thing, Liza. She just fell in and was consumed by it all. It was strange, as if that's what she wanted."

"I miss her, Becky," gulped Liza.

"I know," I whispered and then I began. Liza listened and huge tears swelled up in her eyes but I carried on regardless. I was speaking of things that I hadn't told a living soul. "She didn't scream.

She didn't do a thing. I tried to help. I jumped in after her but I lost her in the blackness. I lost her in the blackness, Liza. It surrounded us, engulfed us. I reached out my hand hoping to touch Megan's but I couldn't feel her. Instead I touched the other side. It's strange - in the blackness there's light and warmth. I saw her."

A salt water stream flowed down her cheeks yet she was awakened by this new sentence and she grew stronger.

"Who?"

"Megan."

"When?"

"While I was ill."

"They said you nearly died."

"I did and that's where I saw her."

"Where?"

"Near a valley which was near a meadow, underneath a rainbow, and she was there by a stream. She looked happy but I couldn't get her attention. Then she got up and over the hill came a bunch of little girls with flowing dresses and pink clouds darting up above their heads."

Liza's forehead was wrinkled; she looked at me with complete and utter bewilderment. "Did some of them have roses on the sleeves?"

I stared back at her with the same bewilderment and quietly whispered "Yes."

"Were you in a field of yellow flowers? Becky, I was right behind you the whole time."

"But I couldn't see you."

"I know. I wasn't like you and Megan. Your feet were on the ground and Megan walked on the land, but I was floating in the air. I thought it was a dream. It was a dream, wasn't it, Becky? `Cause if it wasn't a dream, how did we get there?"

I stared at my poor confused friend. I hadn't the heart to tell her it was real. I let her believe it was a mere dream that somehow both of us had been drawn into; though the place did feel like a dream, for surely no paradise like that could ever possibly exist. Liza and I had felt the same things, witnessed the same event. Both of us had travelled there for the love of Megan. She had taken each of us there. The only difference between Liza and me was I nearly had to die to go there.

I had stayed the longest and had seen too much, thus the price I had paid was considerably more than the confusion that Liza would feel for the rest of her life. My price had been a piece of me, a hole in my mind, and the emptiness came in sudden bursts. Epilepsy had swapped place with my childhood. We had been touched by a child who would remain forever in our hearts. Even if someday we lost our innocence as we walked the path of maturity, just past the crossroads of adulthood, the mere thought of Megan would rekindle those lost emotions.

At this time, though, we had not reached that time of reflection; we were still in the cataclysm of tragedy. I looked at Liza and searched her eyes. What we had seen, and the friend we had shared, brought us back together. I looked at her there in the playground and felt sorry for her. "Liza, tell your mother something from me, will you?"

"What?"

"Tell her that epilepsy isn't catching."

"I'll tell her, Becky, and even if she doesn't let us see each other after school, we can still see each other at playtime and at dinner. Do you want to eat dinner with me?"

"I'm not in the same team as you anymore."

"Yeah, but we still eat packed lunch."

"Aye, we've both still got our teeth."

The bell rang signalling the end of playtime. As I was about to run back into school, my head happened to turn towards the school gates. I saw my mother holding on to the cold iron bars of the gate, looking for all the world like a prisoner trapped and unable to get out.

I walked over to her. "What's the matter?"

She looked to the ground. She seemed embarrassed as if she'd been caught out. "I… I… I came to see if you were alright."

"Aye, I'm fine."

"Good. Good." There was a long silence between us and it somehow pleased me.

"I made friends again with Liza."

"That's great, I'm really glad. If you hadn't, I was gonna go round to Joan and give her a piece of my mind."

"Don't do that, Mum, she doesn't really understand about it. Just talk to her and explain what it actually is."

"Aye, you're right."

"Thanks. I'd better go now."

"Aye you run along now. See you tonight then, Becky." My mother bent down, squeezed her head through the bars of the gate and kissed me.

"See you tonight, Mammy."

"See you later, alligator."

"In a while, crocodile," I yelled, as I ran back to school.

That year I came full circle. I went from the dark into the light. The dark of illness came from within, enticed out of its black den by the light itself. I grew up just a little more than I should have. Responsibility became my constant companion and I was no longer frightened of things I could not see. I lived both in light and in shadow.

In the light of day I did not remember things, but within the deep blackness of night I remembered all too well the emptiness that surrounded me, mirrored in that blackness of the night that encased me with its visions of Megan falling silently. Megan, my friend.

Liza was a friend, or once had been. She was still rather cool towards me but at least her mother let us play together. The haunted house no longer seemed haunted, empty of friends and ghosts yet full of memories. We were too frightened to go into Auntie's house, not because of the ghosts but for fear of seeing ourselves yesterday. I'd look across to Megan's house too; no-one had ever told me what happened to Mrs Doherty.

"What happened?" I nodded towards the house.

"Megan died."

"I know that, but what happened to Mrs Doherty?"

"Didn't your father tell you?"

"No."

"Amazing."

"What do you mean?"

"Nothing." Now Liza had secrets from me. Everybody had secrets from me. She shrugged her shoulders and walked away. "She's gone back to Ireland."

"Will she be coming back?"

"I very much doubt it. I mean, what has she got to come back to?"

We sat on the swings that father had erected in the garden for me, with the strict warning, "Don't go too high." Liza and I sat swaying gently on them. Our legs dangled down and every so often we would dig the earth with our lifeless feet as we rocked from side to side. I stared forlornly at the ground. Then my feet prodded the earth and I noticed something being reflected by the winter sun's rays. I bent down and picked it up.

Liza's eyes followed me. "What is it, Becky?"

"I dunno, it looks like some kind of tooth." I held the cold, white jagged item in the palm of my hand and my fingers picked at it as we both wondered what it was. Its shape suggested it was definitely a tooth but it looked too big to be human. Liza looked at it with wide eyes until they beamed in a 'Eureka' moment.

"It's a dinosaur tooth."

"It's too small to be a dinosaur tooth."

"There were small dinosaurs. Maybe it's a baby dinosaur's tooth."

"How do you know?"

"'Cause I do, that's how."

"Oh!"

"Let's 'ave a gizz at it?"

"No!" My hand shut tight and encased the tooth within my fist, but then suddenly everything went black. There was no sound, no taste, no smell, nothing; shadow had devoured me once again. Without warning it just sprang upon me like a bird of prey, snatching my confidence and self-worth in one fatal swoop.

When colours formed shapes once more and I came to, I noticed my hand was open and the dinosaur tooth had gone and so was Liza. I looked down the garden, the gate was swinging open and I could hear her running. I didn't run after her. It simply wasn't worth it as there was nothing to run after. She'd stolen the tooth and a part of me.

It turned out to be just an old jagged piece of limestone that father had broken off when he put the swings in the garden.

Events had transpired against humanity. Father's blatant embarrassment at having an emotionally disturbed sister had caused him to behave with calculated coldness towards her. His behaviour towards me was also highly questionable. I tried to talk him round to go and see Auntie Maggie but he would hear none of it. He would shoo me away or walk away out of sight so he could no longer see me, now that I had become an embarrassment too. He always appeared so busy and kept out of my way, with lots of school governor meetings to attend even when he was at home. I never saw much of him at all. It was after Liza told me what had happened to Mrs Doherty and her move back to Ireland that I decided to talk to him. One night I pretended to go to sleep when Peter and Leah went to bed, then waited for him on the stairs so I would get him as soon as he walked in the door.

I crept downstairs and sat on the last step waiting for him, staring closely at the door. As I studied it, out of the darkness I began to see a face with deep-set eyes. I tried to see the mouth but the face itself seemed to protrude in a sinister glare. I wanted to see welcoming lips but just saw eyes, a thin nose and an oval face staring at me. It was the face of someone I didn't know, a face I had never seen before but would see many times in the coming years. It would appear in patterns, in wallpaper, in quilt designs, in bathroom tiles and in landscape pictures painted by artists who presumably did not want faces appearing in their works of art.

Suddenly I heard a key rattle its way into the lock, which gave a stark clack, and the door handle began to turn slowly. I sat upright. It was dark in the hall but a moonbeam quickly flashed, lighting the way for the weary fisherman. His bag fell with a thud at the corner nearest the door. His boots were the next thing to be caged nearby.

Then in walked father. He had grown a beard. He stood straight and stretched his back. The moon was right behind him and for a brief moment the light shone all around him. His light blue eyes seem to shine and his dark brown hair had flecks of white in it. He let out a sigh and sharply closed the door, turning round to put the lock on it.

"Father."

"Jesus, Mary and Joseph." He seemed to jump a foot in the air. "Becky, don't do that, darling. I'm not as young as I used to be. I can't take shocks like that anymore."

"I'm sorry."

"What are you doing up so late?"

"I wanted to talk to you."

"Well, you could talk to me tomorrow."

"You might not be here when I wake up."

"I wouldn't do that."

"Yes, you have."

"No, I haven't. I'm sure I'd have remembered doing something like that."

"Well, you've got a short memory then." Realising that I was getting nowhere fast, I tried something else. "Look, I don't want to have an argument with you."

"Thank God for that. I'd hate it for you to turn into your mother."

"She's not so bad now."

Father stared deeply at me for several moments. "It's late, Becky, you should go to bed." Those were the words that broke the silence. He wanted to get rid of me.

"Do I embarrass you as much as Auntie Maggie?"

"What?"

"You heard. Are you ashamed of us?" I often wondered what he saw when he looked in the mirror.

"I'm not ashamed of you."

"No?"

"No."

"And what about my Auntie Maggie?"

"Don't keep calling her Auntie. She's not."

"She's your sister, isn't she?" There was no answer. "Then she's my auntie."

"Becky, please, you'll make yourself ill. Go on to bed, there's a good girl."

"No."

"What?"

"No, I won't be brushed aside. I'm tired of living in lies and secrets. Your lies, your secrets. People whispering behind my back. Everybody knows what's going on except me. And I still don't know what happened."

"What do you mean?"

"To Megan, Mrs Doherty, Maggie."

"Maggie's gone to a place where they can give her the attention she needs."

"She doesn't need that kind of attention. All she needs is some attention from her family and she'll be alright."

"You don't understand, Becky."

"No, I don't."

"I don't expect you to."

"Why?" Father was silent. "Why? Is it because you think I'm too stupid to understand? I'm not capable of seeing how narrow-minded you are?"

Father stood there with one hand holding onto the banister rail, looking like he was about to collapse. But I had to get what I wanted to say off my chest. I was none the wiser, I had no answers but I felt better. I stood up and turned to walk back to my room but then father tried to have one last word. His voice was quiet and shaky.

"Well, you have become your mother. I thought you and I were the same, Becky. I thought you were like my side of the family, not your mother's."

"No, father, I'm not like you and your side of the family. The side of stuck-up Siobvon and the cruel and jealous cousins. And I'm not like mother. I'm like no-one. I'm the one who doesn't fit in. I try to but there's nothing left for me. Goodnight."

And I left him there at the bottom of the stairs. I never turned round as I went to my room. Leah had crept into my bedroom and was waiting for me.

"How do you feel?"

"Better."

"No doubt, getting all that off your chest. You were really something, Becky."

"Me? Do you think?"

"Yeah! You were great, little sister." And Leah put her arms round me.

"Do you think Mammy heard me?"

"I think the whole bloody avenue heard you."

I squeezed my sister tighter as we laughed together that night before falling asleep, telling each other stories of Christmases we had endured and wondering what this Christmas would bring.

—NINETEEN—

I recalled how last year I had not wanted to leave Megan and Liza. It would have been our first Christmas together, and little did I know then that it would have been our last. Last year, I had fought my parents long and hard about going to Ireland; this year they decided it was best that we stayed home. But I really wanted to leave. I really wanted to get away.

Just before Christmas, father came home and the Christmas Miracle was beginning to blossom again. We sat at the table eating and talking together, not screaming. Mother was adamant that we were most definitely not going to Ireland.

"But why?"

"Because."

"Because what?"

"Because you're not ready to travel yet, Rebekah."

"Rhubarb."

"Rebekah!" It was father. My outcry was not permitted. Peter and Leah looked on in silence as I tried again with mother.

"But why?"

"Because you're still ill, Rebekah, that's why."

"I've been at school for the past month and nothing has happened. I haven't dropped down dead or anything."

"Oh, Rebekah, stop being so morbid."

"I can't help it, Mammy dear, it's the Irish in me." To this she said nothing and continued to talk with father, who had decided to ignore me as well. Peter leaned forward towards me.

"They're not listening, Miss Four Leaf Clover."

Leah moved closer. "They pretend not to when you've said something relevant."

"What does 'relevant' mean?"

"Something they know is true."

I had nothing to fear from Peter and Leah anymore, for they had become my friends and allies. Peter especially never left my side. He watched me constantly, his eyes following me everywhere and he was always two steps in front. While I was in the bath, either my mother or Leah would sit and watch me. My mother made sure that I was never left on my own and I was not allowed to be bored. She made me read things to her. My days were spent at school reading, writing and learning and so were my evenings.

I didn't mind the days so much because I learned the guitar with Mrs Temple, who had bought me a guitar as a gift. And I was not the only child she taught; in fact we were a quartet and I thought we would be victimised but actually no-one said a word. Maybe that was because we were slightly different to the rest of the school and from difference comes fear of the unknown. Two of my guitar-playing friends had learning disabilities, one with dyslexia and the other was terrible in every class he'd been in and was forever being sent out to Mrs Temple. The other teachers couldn't stand David and pleaded with Mrs Temple to send him away to a special school for 'maladjusted' children. But she refused and took it upon herself to teach him. Miss Pike called him Satan's Child but within out little quartet David was a saint; he even played the guitar better than Mrs Temple. Last in our group was Michael who had Multiple Sclerosis. None of us knew exactly what that meant but we figured it must be something serious as he had his own nurse with him constantly.

Our quartet was practising for the Christmas play. Mrs Temple had organised the whole school to study how Christmas is celebrated in other countries. Each class would have a ten-minute slot in the special Assembly when they would tell all those present, such as parents, teachers and friends, everything they knew about their chosen country's rituals. The quartet would play along to the carols as the classes sang in their country's language. We were the pride of Mrs Temple and by the time the Christmas Assembly came round we had spent more time with her than our own teachers. We did not care but I had the distinct feeling that Suki and company did.

All the parents congregated in the hall chattering nervously to one another about their child's achievements, while secretly praying it would not be their child to run off the stage crying. Meanwhile the children were just as nervous, chattering anxiously to each other in their classrooms while getting ready for their parts. The players, as the quartet was called, wandered from classroom to classroom looking and touching and generally making a nuisance of ourselves, as was of course expected of us. It was while I was doing my rounds that I met Suki and Katie.

"Oh, hi Rebekah."

"Hello."

"What are you doing here?"

"Me? I'm just looking round."

"Yes, we've been looking round as well, haven't we, Katie?"

"Yes. Definitely." Their eyes glistened with mischief.

"Oh, that's nice," I mumbled and quickly sidled away from their destructive envy. I wondered what exactly what they had been up to, but I didn't have to wait long.

I turned round to see Mrs Temple signalling for me to come. The other members of the quartet were with her. She then ushered us into the hall and we took our places on the stage. Mrs Temple introduced us and told the parents a little about what was to happen.

The parents clapped as the first victims – sorry, class - came into the hall. Mrs Temple took her place at the piano so that when she was needed she could play along with us or give a solo.

In this class were Katie, Suki and Carly; their chosen country was Germany and their first song was O Christmas Tree. I was to start first. Everything went quiet as the parents settled down and Suki and Katie turned their heads to me, waiting for me to begin. I put my fingers into position and struck the guitar. The strings snapping one by one was the only sound to be heard as parents held their breath. I looked up to see their faces peering at me and then saw Katie and Suki with their eyes full of laughter. It was Carly who gave out the first huge cry of laughter and then a cascade of glee followed. I couldn't stand it, threw down my guitar and ran out with my parents in hot pursuit.

The rest of the evening proceeded the way it had begun. Halfway through, sets had fallen down, costumes fell to pieces and Nigel and Phillip Mathewson had started fighting. Mrs Temple apparently had a whale of time, throwing her hands in the air and laughing until she cried. The only word she could utter that evening was "Fabulous". However, Miss Pike was not amused.

Mrs Temple was my saviour at school. She often brought me little marzipan figures. I didn't have the heart to tell her that I was not keen on marzipan but because she had bought them for me I devoured them with relish and decided they tasted divine.

Much to my pleasure, she also did not like Miss Pike and tried every trick in the book to annoy her. During the Christmas Term Mrs Temple had ordered that every classroom be decorated. Miss Pike did not participate and felt that this year's display of garden slugs was quite sufficient so she was quite surprised to walk into her classroom one Monday morning to find that Mrs Temple had been in over the weekend to decorate it. She had put tinsel round the blackboard and shiny lights round the garden slugs' tank. In the middle of their made-up garden stood a plastic snowman. Mrs Temple thought it looked "T'riffic" while Miss Pike was not amused.

For her part, Miss Pike did her utmost to try and bind chains round "the free spirit so typical of the Irish". Thus I had a large amount of work to do in the classroom as she figured that if I were kept busy and had discipline imposed upon me permanently, I "might turn out to be a remotely interesting human being in later life". This was probably one of the greatest compliments that Miss Pike ever gave me. Among my chores was tidying out the Play Corner, not that we ever did play in Miss Pike's class. It was also my job to mix the paints for everyone as well as to wash the brushes and clear things away when we had finished with them. I had to do all this as well as my work in class: Maths, English, Science, reading and handwriting practice could not be left half-finished. So I became the quickest in the class at finishing work.

There were days when I felt ill, as if I were in a bubble. Normal life was going on around me but I could not join in, for I felt disjointed in some way. The things I did on those days were slow, heavy and difficult. It was as if I were moving in slow motion yet the rest of the world carried on as normal. People talked and I would listen, I would do whatever they asked and what was normal but emotions did not come into it. Whatever I touched, I could not feel.

At dinner time I would do the same as always and go to the playground waiting for the older classes to finish dinner. I would even play some games but never actually took part. When finally we went for our dinner I sat in the same place and talked about what people had to eat, but whatever I ate I didn't taste. It was not surprising that people never noticed anything different about me, but I was disengaged from others' reality.

I was somehow switched to automatic, disconnected, encased like Megan had been, as if a piece of glass surrounded me. I saw the world going on out there but inside it was just me and my thoughts. Sometimes the glass barrier would be shattered by emotions into a thousand pieces, jagged and hard, so sharp that they seemed to cut deep enough for the flesh to bleed. Then emotions, feelings and tastes became entombed in my inner world, leaving me weak, my stomach heavy.

When at last I arrived home I would vomit constantly and the night would be full of images of horror streaming through my mind. Sorrow and loss mixed with the dull throbbing pain of my mind kept me awake all night. The pain and images would get worse at that certain time somewhere between night and day, a time when words have no meaning. Then all of a sudden it would come sweeping in on a silent, serene wave as dancing light heralded the dawn of a new day. A beam of light would stretch through the gap in my curtains at the top of the window, bouncing through curtains of flowers and clouds. It would yawn and spiral down to the floor where it lay still and dead, the dance over.

The light of the sun that had warmed the streets where we played our games now suddenly disappeared. My childhood was frozen. I would close my eyes and finally sleep. But it was impossible for me even to attempt to go to school after I had had such a night. Miss Pike and others would claim that I was pretending to be ill on my days off, using the excuse that I was perfectly well the day before. But they never bothered to ask if I were ill or well.

There was a small gathering of snow one morning and everywhere looked clean. For a brief respite, the town streets looked pure as if for a moment nature had forgiven the people who walked those streets with their heads down. Even Auntie Maggie's oak tree echoed a momentary happiness that had not been felt since the summer when we had played under its shade. The night had been so cold that my head pounded with the pain from the harsh air in my room. I pulled the blankets up round me and tried to put the covers up over my head but my breath got shorter and shorter, so I pulled the covers away and arose gulping for air.

"Are you alright?" Leah murmured.

"Aye. My head's cold, though. I'm trying to get it warm but I keep suffocating instead."

"Put a hat on then."

"They're all downstairs."

"Oh well, we'll be getting up soon. We're going Christmas shopping with Mammy."

"That should be an experience," I replied, while balancing the pillow on my head.

Mother's shopping trips were quite something. She found fault with every display in every window, in every shop. Every time she would go inside the shop to look around then ask to see the manager and complain to him not only about his window display but also about something else in the store she did not agree with. Suffice to say, my shopping trips with mother were few and far between.

This one I was quite dreading. It was not just our first Christmas in England but our first Christmas shopping trip to the posh part of town as a family. I had really avoided that part of town, and come to think of it so had Peter and Leah. The last time I was there was when I had gone with father for my school uniform and that seemed a world ago. We arrived early in the morning. Everything was indoors so I could at least take off my gloves but was ordered not to dare loosen my coat and in no circumstances take off my hat. Father and Peter were given instructions on where and when to meet, what to buy and what not to buy and how much to spend, while Leah and myself were dragged round by mother.

Everything was so busy. I didn't look up for fear of bumping into someone so I never saw people's faces, only their legs and shoes. It was while mother was complaining to a store manager that I saw him. I was standing alone outside the shop when, through the busy crowds shoving and pushing, my eyes fell upon a young boy about the same age as me. He was in a wheelchair and my eyes focused on his legs, covered by a thin pair of trousers. Through them I could see the shape of undeveloped human bones, his legs so short. His mother fussed round him pointing things out, but she never showed him the young girl swallowing the tears that filled her eyes at the sight of him. I blinked a couple of times to pretend there was something in my eyes, afraid that people near me would see me cry, but they never noticed me and they never noticed him. His legs were in the wheelchair as if they had been clumsily placed on him; they couldn't even carry a hair on his head, but would snap under the weight. I felt my legs beneath me, strong enough to carry me, and I felt the ground underneath my feet as I walked, tall and firm.

I was so grateful to be who I am, what I am, and to have what I have. Yet I felt terribly sad for him. He would never know the ground beneath his feet or the sand between his toes on a warm, sunny beach. His body could never dance to a rhythm that moves the soul and I wondered if music would ever play for him the way it played for me, the way it moved me. My strong legs could carry my body as my soul danced the dance of freedom, the dance that only the soul knows. I prayed that one day his soul would dance for freedom as well.

Where was the sense of it all? What was the reason? Why was I born with these strong columns and he born with twigs for legs that would snap if they tried to carry his equally fragile body? But at least, I thought, he has never felt strong legs; they were never snatched away from him. At least he has eyes to see the colours and beauty around him. At least he can hear the loving words greeting him. At least he can feel the wind upon his face. At least he can see the waves rolling in and hear them crash upon the shore. At least… shadow swooped down and everything went black. When I realised where I was, he had gone and my mother was kneeling beside me.

"Are you alright? It's all been bit much, let's get home. Now, where's your bastard father?"

"Don't get on at Daddy, Mammy. It's not his fault," Leah said as she helped me up. But mother was already off searching for father. We went home early. I had wanted to get away from it all. I just wanted peace and calm. But that was not to be.

Christmas Eve had the same effect on my brother and sister as always. They were scurrying round the house all night. Mother, in her infinite wisdom, had decided that we could open one present each but the rest had to wait until Christmas Day. She gave Peter and Leah their presents and then hurried into the kitchen to check on her Christmas pudding; she was steaming most of it now and then would finish the rest tomorrow. Mother was in charge of Christmas, now that she no longer had to wait for Aunt Siobvon to declare Christmas open.

In the corner was a familiar square package. I sighed and turned to Leah who was trying her present on, repeatedly asking me what I thought and decidedly not content with "It's alright".

"Becky, what do you think? It's me, isn't it? Do you think Mark will like it?"

"Who's Mark?"

"No-one." She winked at me.

"Yes, it's lovely, Leah. It really enhances your eyes."

"Cheers, Becky. Oh, I got you a special prezzie."

"You did? What is it?"

"You'll have to open it." Leah handed me a present that she had bought and wrapped herself. It was soft and… "Well go on, bloody open it. Don't try guessing it."

"But that's half the fun." I began to rip the paper and suddenly bright colours of the most vomiting variety abused my eyes. "What the hell is this?"

"It's a hat - for your head."

"Well, you'd hardly put it on your arse, would you?"

"Thank you, Peter, for those wise words. Well, try it on," Leah urged proudly.

I held the abomination in my hands. "Are you visually impaired, Leah?"

"No."

"Are you colour blind?"

"No."

"Well, you bloody will be if you look at this long enough."

"Oh, go on with ya. There's nothing wrong with it. It'll do the job it's supposed to." Leah grabbed the hat-thing out of my hand and plopped it on my head. She tugged and pulled at it until she was satisfied. "There now, isn't that grand?"

I looked in the mirror. "Aye, but I won't wear it outside."

"Why not?"

"Well, in case it might offend someone."

Peter nearly choked on his smuggled chocolate. Mother had instructed us not to eat any chocolate over Christmas as she believed it would make us sick due to all the rich food Christmas brings. Yet somehow Peter had managed to sneak chocolate bars upstairs without her finding out. I have no idea how he got away with it, especially when mother cleaned our rooms. Her cleaning always consisted of checking under mattresses, in drawers and wardrobes, anywhere that something could be hidden. She did this ritual at least once a week. She kept secrets from us yet hated her children to have any secrets of their own, to keep her in the dark. We were not allowed to hide anything from her. Her fanatical contradictions were a complete mystery to me.

That night I tossed and turned. I was so cold and my head was throbbing, my nose was frozen and I could no longer feel my ears. In the end I got out of bed and put Leah's hat on my head. I would not wear it outside but it did keep my head warm inside. I simply could not bear the pain of the cold on my head.

"Great prezzie, Leah. It really keeps my head warm," I whispered into the night.

"That was the idea, little sister."

"Thank you, Leah."

"You're welcome, little one."

—TWENTY—

So far, Christmas in England had been a mixture of crap and dull. The loss of Megan and Liza was almost unbearable and had it not been for my sister and brother I don't think I would have come downstairs at all. As usual, they were up at the crack of dawn and wanted to open my presents too, with declarations of concern for my strength and welfare. By the time I did arrive downstairs, wearing the hat-thing, or thing-hat, Leah was already dressing up in more new clothes and Peter had already broken one of his games.

Mother and father were cooking together. But despite threats made with the carving knife and boiling carrot water, it was actually going rather smoothly. Mother spotted me from the kitchen where she seemed to be about to impale father with several meat skewers.

"Ah, there you are. I was beginning to think we'd have to send a search and rescue party up to your room. Sleep well?"

"No."

"Good. Well… well, doesn't Leah's hat look fine on you?"

"No."

"Well, close your eyes. Santa's present is all ready and waiting for you."

"Oh, not more books. Santa must think I'm very studious."

"Be quiet now. Sean?"

Father was summoned from the kitchen. At least she used his name, the name he had been baptised with in a church, not the one mother had re-christened him. But then, the Christmas Miracle was at work and mother and father were both surpassing themselves in cordiality. And for the first time in my life, Santa got me what I'd always wanted, albeit a year late.

"Peter, go and help your father bring in Becky's present. Be careful he doesn't knock the wallpaper, now."

Peter swallowed his chocolate, obediently got up from in front of the telly and walked past mother.

"Have you been eating chocolate?"

"No Mammy," he gulped. "I'm waiting for my dinner. I know how much dinner means to you."

"Creep," Leah sneezed. Peter and father struggled with something out in the yard.

"Now, you sit down there and close your eyes." She placed me in a chair. My eyes were tightly shut. "No peeking now, I want this to be surprise. Oh, you'll never dream what it could be." I heard a bell ring as Peter and father struggled closer and closer.

"Go on, Becky. You can open your eyes now."

I feared to open them but I had a sneaky suspicion when the bell ring gave it away. And... yes, it was a bike. "Wow. Thank you, Santa."

"At least he got something right this time, eh?" Peter nudged me.

"Well, I did want a BMX."

"Oh no, that's far too sporty for you."

"Aye, you might hurt yourself on it," Peter agreed with Leah. "There's nothing wrong with this one, is there?"

"No, it's great. Can I try it out?"

"Yes," said father.

"No, not today," mother got in, while father stared at her. "It's a bit cold. And you're not dressed. You haven't had your breakfast. And dinner will be ready soon. And it gets dark so early."

I felt like screaming. "Okay, so tomorrow maybe?"

"Maybe. But you've got all the time in the world to play on it. And I'm sure Leah and Peter will go with you."

Peter quickly backed her up. "Oh yeah. Sure. Absolutely. Whenever."

"Good. Well, that's all done. Come on Sean, back to the kitchen and you'd better cook those chestnuts right this time."

After dinner we all felt sufficiently sick. Mother was sprawled out on an armchair with her feet propped up on the coffee table, sleeping soundly, safe in the knowledge that she had made Christmas and Aunt Siobvon was well and truly redundant.

"No honestly, Leah, you're not fat."

"Are you sure? I mean, that meal must have put at least an inch on me. I know you're just trying to be nice, Becky, but I daren't try any clothes on, I might split them."

"Well, go running then," moaned Peter from the floor, where he lay putting the final pieces in his jigsaw.

"That's a good idea. Exercise Leah, that's what you need. Tell you what, why don't we go to the park? I can ride my bike and you can run alongside me."

Father raised an eyebrow. "You heard what your Mammy said, Rebekah, she doesn't want you to go out today."

"But I'm alright. I want to play on my bike. And Leah's coming with me."

Peter jumped up. "I'll go as well. Come on, let's go."

"Now wait a minute, boy. I didn't say you could. What about your mother?"

"You can tell her where we've gone."

"It's not that easy, Leah."

"Well, why don't you come with us, then? You could just leave a note for her."

With that idea in mind father sprang from his chair. "Alright, let's go."

His children looked at one another with disbelief while he got the note paper. We were amazed to be going out with our father. Peter especially appeared baffled; he couldn't work it out. Father carried my bike out of the door while Leah bounced along the hall, 'warming up'. With the racket she made, I'm amazed mother didn't wake up.

And so a family made its way to the park, a father and his children spending Christmas Day afternoon walking off the rich food. To all intents and purposes, I suppose we looked perfect. Father was proud. Peter walked near me as I nervously wobbled down the street on my new bike. Leah jogged next to father a little behind Peter and me. Obediently, we stopped at every road and waited for father to cross with us. How perfect. A perfect lie.

I had not forgotten Aunt Maggie and I desperately wanted to see her. While riding my bike, I began to think about her and ideas of how I could get to see her raced round and round my head. We reached the park and… blackness. Shadow swept over me. When I realised what was happening, we were back home.

"I told you she wasn't allowed out today."

"Oh, for Christ's sake, it's Christmas. She wanted to play on her bike."

"I told you we shouldn't have bought it. I - "

"Oh, do be quiet, you two."

The adults were not amused.

"Where's Peter and Leah?"

"They've gone back out again."

"I want to go."

"No, Rebekah, you're going to lie down."

"No, I want to go on my bike."

"You need to sleep for a bit. Come on, let's get you upstairs to bed."

"No, I don't want your help." I pushed my mother away and father stepped in. "I don't want your bloody help either."

"Rebekah, your father carried you home."

"I didn't ask him to. And where's my bike?"

"Leah's on it, cycling round the park with Peter jogging beside her."

"That's not fair. I want my bike. Go get my bike back. It's my bike," I moaned to father, pushing him towards the door. He looked at mother with wonder.

"Go on, Sean, do as she says," mother answered him. I watched him go out of the front door. "Now, come on you, let's get up the stairs."

"Leave me alone. I can manage."

With pain all through my head, the dull throb in the centre permeated the sharp running pain, to and fro. I seemed to be going slowly and treading heavily up the stairs, even though my anger thought I was stomping up. Eventually I got to my bedroom door and reached out my hand. I saw my hand grip the handle but I did not register the feeling. I turned the door handle as it seemed the right thing to do. The door opened and I knew I had to walk into the room where I saw my bed next to the wall, looking so inviting. But it was still light outside and I wanted to go out.

I turned round to face the door and I knew I had to close it. I reached out my hand again and touched the handle; I had gripped it before, yes, I had to hold it. So I folded my sweaty hand round the handle and walked closer until my nose pressed against the door, then continued walking and the door shut. I released my grip and turned round again. The bed was still there, still looking inviting. I looked at the window; it was still light and I still wanted to go out and I still wasn't allowed.

I wanted to play with my friends. What friends? Megan had gone, she had new friends now. I wondered if she would remember me when we met again, as I felt we would. Liza had changed towards me and as for the Pink Brigade, well, they had forgotten the games we'd played with Megan. Megan was probably an embarrassment for them. No doubt they'd say they felt sorry for her and that's why they played with her.

I looked at the dressing table where Aunt Siobvon's dolls were elegantly arranged. My Megan had place of honour, standing in the middle, straight and perfect. Her red hair fell below her waist and green bonnet hid part of her curls. I moved from where I had been standing for the past several minutes and walked to the dressing table. I saw my reflection but didn't know who was staring back. I had brown hair, that figure had brown hair and looked so pale, tired and sick. I looked away, not bearing to see my reflection in my eyes any longer.

I reached my hand out and took hold of Megan. I stroked her red hair, twisted it round my fingers and made more curls. I took the bonnet off and brushed the hair away from her face. Her painted features were meticulously drawn. I followed the shape of her nose with my finger and felt the dead coldness of her beauty. I felt…

I fell.

Blackness swooped down upon me again. The shadow had awoken and decided to come out. When I came to, Megan was still in my hand though I was lying on the floor. I moved so that I could see Megan. Her painted features had gone; there was just a hole left and her crumpled body clattered in my hand.

Mother came bounding in. "Oh my God, what's happened? You've had a fit, haven't you?"

"It's not fits, it's a dizzy spell," I mumbled automatically.

"See, I told you you weren't allowed to go out. And I was right. Your father doesn't understand these things like I do. What do you think would have happened if you'd gone out on your own with your bike? You might have fell in the street or in front of a car and what would have happened then? I dread to think."

"Then don't."

"Come on, let's get you into bed. What have we here?" Mother prized Megan out of my hand that still clutched her. "Oh dear, you must have banged her head on the dressing table when you fell. What a shame. But I'm sure Aunt Siobvon will buy you another one for Christmas. We didn't get round to opening all the presents but I'm sure she will have. The postman brought a parcel for you a couple of weeks ago. It's bound to be a doll from Siobvon. The old bitch always does buy you one. I'll throw this one away."

"No." I snatched back my Megan with all the strength that was left in me. "No. You're not taking her away."

"But it's all broken and you've got a dozen others to choose from."

"I don't want them, I want this one." And I clutched her so tight I thought the rest of her would break.

"Oh, you're bloody awkward. Now come on into bed."

Mother got me into bed and I held Megan all the time I was awake; even while I was vomiting I didn't let her go.

She is the only doll I ever kept; I gave the others away when I grew up. But I still kept Megan, my doll with no face and a broken body tied together with bits of string and elastic bands. To me she was still the prettiest of all the dolls Aunt Siobvon gave me. She now lives in a battered shoe box that is entitled My Childhood, with bits and pieces, pictures I'd drawn and poems I had written. There was an embroidered cushion cover I made at school but never got round to filling and a picture of an owl I drew when I was eleven. Broken

Megan lay on the top, my doll with no face and a battered old faded dress. When I look at it I still remember the summer I met Megan, sitting on her garden wall waiting for her mother to take her to church.

Christmas Day was nearly over when I finally woke up. Everywhere was in darkness and I couldn't hear any voices from downstairs either. I lay in bed staring into the darkness, wondering if I moved my head to get up would the shadow sweep over me again. In the end I couldn't stand any more thoughts and gradually allowed myself to rise up, slowly at first, until I was sitting upright in bed. So far so good. I moved my legs out of bed and sat waiting, then just got up. I stood still. The room seemed to sway a little from side to side but there was still no shadow. The door was difficult to find in the darkness but I didn't want to put the light on. I reached for the wall and fell towards it, but my hands broke the fall. Still no shadow. I ran my hands along the wall until at last they touched the door handle. I pulled it open and found myself still in complete darkness.

I would not attempt the stairs without the light on, so after finding it near the bathroom I ventured down into the mouth of silent darkness. I opened the living room door and let my eyes grow accustomed to the night once more. The television was off, there was nothing, but I knew someone was there. I thought I saw an outline of someone in the corner.

"Hello," I dared to say.

"Hello, little girl." And with that, father switched the light on.

"What are you doing sitting in the dark?"

"I like the dark. It reminds me of when I'm out at sea and there's complete nothingness."

"Too much to remember, eh?"

"I like to think of nothing," was the reply.

I stood in the doorway and he sat in the light. He looked uncomfortable despite the huge cushions almost swallowing him. Something was wrong. In the end, he broke the silence. I had no desire to do that for him.

"Are you happy, little girl?"

"What kind of a question is that?"

"I'm just being polite, making conversation with my little girl."

"I'm not your little girl."

"Oh, yes you are."

"I've got epilepsy remember? I've got something wrong with me."

"Don't be ridiculous, you'll grow out of it. It's not like Mag - " He stopped himself before completing Auntie's name.

"You can't even bear to hear yourself say her name, can you?"

"You're not like her. You don't howl."

"What?"

"Nothing, forget that. I didn't say anything."

"Yes, you did."

"Forget it, I said! I've just about had it with you and your cheek, young lady."

I had angered him. I stood quietly at the door, motionless, unsure what to do. He was uncomfortable. Do I go back to bed or do I persevere with what I call 'father'?

"Where is everyone?" I finally asked in a low voice.

Father let out a deep sigh. "To visit your Aunt Maggie."

"So she's near then?"

"Yes."

"Why didn't they take me? You all know how much I want to see her."

"You were ill, remember?"

"When did they go? Are they going to see her again? "

"Knowing your mother, they probably will." I looked puzzled. "Your mother insists on seeing her. She takes Leah and Peter with her, I think more than anything out of companionship."

"Will she take me?"

"No, I don't think so."

"Why?"

"She's probably waiting for me to do that."

"When will we go? We could go for New Year's Day." My hopes were raised but just as swiftly dashed.

"No, no, no, Rebekah! When will you ever listen? No, little girl, I will never take you to see Margaret."

"Her name is Auntie Maggie and I will see her."

Father sprang out of the chair like a coiled snake at its prey. "Up to your room and stay there."

"My pleasure!" I swiftly turned on my heels and leaped up the stairs with such a fire burning inside. I could feel the strength surging through my veins. I slammed my door shut. I don't know why, but I had the feeling I had won.

Father never did take me to see Auntie Maggie, so at least for once he was true to his word. Nevertheless, I knew now that Auntie could not be that far away, somewhere in the town. I'd thought father had sent her back to Ireland.

I never really knew what my parents' war was about or how it started. All I do know is that when the events that changed all our lives forever happened, my mother wanted to care for Aunt Maggie. It was the ammunition she wanted, the perfect weapon to destroy father completely. Poor father could find no solace anywhere now, not even in work. The Cod Wars had destroyed what was left of great-grandfather's fleet; father had to sell them to make ends meet and he was left with just the Rachel Marie.

Not one member of my immediate family ever told me what had happened after Auntie had saved me. Instead, it was the family doctor who did, when I was older. That summer, it was said that

Maggie had made real progress, so much so that her mood swings were not as erratic and she was able to talk about her family. Then on the day I went to see father with Megan, a storm was brewing. It was to become one of the greatest storms we'd ever had, and pictures of a tornado hovering over the estuary were seen in the local paper. Apparently I was awake when father and the other fishermen dragged me from the sea. My eyes were open and for that reason they didn't call an ambulance, but I was not awake. Tony Quinn drove us home and dropped Maggie off while father took me into the house. I even had a bath but I don't remember it.

By now the storm was fast approaching and you could hear the angry rumbles of it in the distance. The wind suddenly rose up and crashed waves into the town. Lightning, it is said, lit the sky in beautiful colours before sending the town into complete darkness with a blackout that lasted almost a day. People were told to stay at home as it was dangerous to venture outside. But by then I was too ill to be moved anyway.

While I lay somewhere in between life and death, the heavens descended upon the town creating a Hell of lightning and the thunder, wind and rain. Oh, how I feel for Aunt Maggie in that house all on her own, surrounded by lies and hate with no-one to talk to and no-one to hold through a night such as that. The only friend she had left lay drifting in and out of death, a few doors down the avenue. But she could not knock on our door. There would be no welcome for her. Is it any wonder she reacted the way she did?

It was when father went to get Doctor Daniels that he also went to see Maggie. I have no idea what was said between sister and brother, but all I know is that twenty years later he has still never seen her. It was some time after father had visited her that it happened. The storm still raged yet people in the nearby houses began to hear a strange sound coming from outside, like an animal in pain howling with fear. The emergency services were already stretched due to the storm. There was no-one to call about this strange noise that seemed to emanate from the old Doen's house. The howling was a human being, a soul reaching out for help - but none was coming. It was a woman's cry of pain at its most fundamental, stemming from emptiness, anguish, loss and seclusion from love and respect. Her howls were the outcries of need for just another human's touch to show that someone cared. But none was coming.

She ran to the door several times but did not open it. Her howls grew fainter as her strength trickled down her face, the blood of life seeping away. The people in their houses breathed a sigh of relief when the howling stopped. She was near to death when they finally found her. Father, in his brutal shame, asked the doctor to put her out of her misery, the way someone would for an animal that was suffering. When she awoke in the psychiatric ward of the hospital, her hands and feet were strapped to the bed, her life bound by leather ties. There she stayed for some time. Had it not been for mother going to see her one day of the week, she would have had no visitors. Her brother would never go.

After seven months she was moved to a Rest Home with people who would care for her for the next twenty years. In the last months of her life she came to live with me. I brought her home and we went swimming every day. It was the childhood that both of us should have had.

But for now my so-called childhood had not yet passed. Revenge had not yet taken its toll.

—TWENTY-ONE—

It was half-way through the Easter Term that Suki was sent back down to Miss Pike's class. It emerged that all this time Suki had been looking over her shoulder at Katie's work, and as Katie was never usually wrong it was hard for the teachers to spot. But when Katie became stuck with algebra, the teachers put two and two together and came up with 'x' - extraordinary copycat. So Suki was sent back to her old class. Miss Pike was rather upset though the only thing she said was, "Oh Suki, I'm so disappointed in you. I thought you knew better."

Suki was amazed at the amount of work I did. I was even more amazed at which group she was put into - Liza's. They seemed to get on very well. No doubt Suki thought she had found another copying book, though this one would be shut to her.

I recalled that the previous summer, just before we split for the holidays, the only thing that had consoled Liza and me was the fact that we would not have to put up with the Pink Team anymore (playing with them in the streets alongside Megan was different). It was hard for me now as I had lost Megan; at least before I could always go to her after school, read her a story and within her silence feel secure. But that summer I had lost not just one friend but two, as Liza had proved when she stole the dinosaur tooth and our friendship. I had no other friends in the class either, as they didn't know how to treat me. I was on my own.

In odd moments, Liza would ask about my illness.

"What's it like?"

"Don't know, it's hard to explain."

"What's your medicine like?"

"Horrible, it's really sweet and it sets your teeth fluttering like mad. It's bad for your teeth."

"Yeah?"

"Yeah. I prefer space dust."

"Oh!"

It seems ironic now that it was Crime Prevention Week but all I can say in my defence is that it was an impulse, sheer impulse with maybe a little revenge thrown in for good measure… Little did I know how eventful dinner time was going to be or, indeed, how the afternoon was to change me forever.

PC Perkins had been round the school showing short cartoon films about a boy playing on a swing and someone offering him sweets and then trying to take him away; but the boy screams and in true cartoon genre his mouth widens so much that you see his tonsils wobbling. Thankfully I was spared this as Miss Pike shut all the blinds in the classroom and turned off all the lights, making the room dark to watch the television. She turned my way and said, "All those of us who are unable to watch television in the dark, for reasons too mediocre to discuss, should leave now." I felt twenty-eight pairs of eyes burning on me, including PC Plod's, so I immediately got up and walked out of the classroom.

I hovered round the cloakroom wondering what I could do when Mrs Temple walked past. I thought I'd make myself invisible among the coats then jump out at her, but Mrs Temple was too quick for me.

"Becky, dear, how are you?"

"I'm hanging in there." I nodded to the coats, hanging up.

"Oh yes, rather good. But what are you doing out here, child? What has Miss Pike been up to now?"

"Oh nothing, they're watching telly and I can't watch it in the dark."

"Oh, yes." She paused and thought. "Miss Pike didn't arrange anything for you to do?"

"No."

"Oh, well why don't you come along with me and help to water the plants?"

I could not resist and I put my small sweaty hand out; her cool fingers folded around it. "Okay," I replied, and we walked down the cloakroom. "I like plants."

"I thought you would, Becky."

The rest of the morning was spent helping Mrs Temple with her plants. We took the dead leaves off together and she showed me that some plants like to have their leaves washed with milk. Mrs Temple was a wonder. She drew me out without me realising. I talked to her about anything and everything, and what was more important was that she listened when no others heard. That morning though, our conversation stayed with plants and Mrs Temple really let me blossom.

"Aren't they lovely, plants?"

"Yes, Becky, they are."

"They're so gentle and delicate."

"Yes, though not all of them are."

"Aren't they?"

"No. There are plants that are meat eaters."

"You're pulling my leg."

"I most certainly am not. You wouldn't have a leg to stand on."

"Well, I would be on my last leg."

"You definitely wouldn't be able to shake a leg."

"This conversation is getting to be too much so I think we'd better leg it."

We both laughed and I looked at the harmless geranium leaf I was holding in my hand; thinking of it as a wild and ferocious, blood-loving meat-eater somehow did not feel quite right. Mrs Temple saw me pondering over this.

"You see, Becky, some plants need meat to survive. They look the same as any other plant and they attract just as many insects."

"Well, they'd have to. I mean, if they didn't they'd go hungry."

"That's absolutely right, Becky. There's one plant in particular called the Venus Fly Trap with leaves like wide opened jaws. When a fly is attracted by its leaves, it flies onto them going deeper and deeper into the mouth. Meanwhile the jaws are closing in on the fly and then they shut tight and the fly is trapped."

"Yuk!"

"Yes, quite right."

"What's the name again?"

"Venus Fly Trap."

"Oh, thanks."

Mrs Temple was reflecting on something and I stared at her expectantly. "I wonder why they called it that."

"Well, it traps flies, Mrs Temple."

"Yes, but why 'Venus', when Venus is the goddess of love?" I could see by the puzzled look on her face that this really bothered her, but I thought the answer was pretty obvious.

"Love hurts."

Mrs Temple's eyes widened. "Why Becky, you are clever."

The dinner bell screamed out and I left Mrs Temple holding the watering can and dreaming about Venus. I ran back to the cloak-room to wait for my class to come out. Suki had well and truly integrated herself within our group, so much so that she even had a packed lunch now. As always the packed lunches sat around their table discussing which chocolate biscuit they had while the dinner ladies fussed round.

All was normal until there was an almighty scream. Everyone looked around and we saw one of our dinner ladies lying on the floor, nursing her ankle. The others flocked round her with cries of "What happened, Pam?" and "Are you alright, love?" Everyone had stopped eating and no-one uttered a word; even Suki looked concerned for once. In the end there was nothing else the dinner ladies could do except call for an ambulance. I noticed some kind of yellow, lumpy substance on the floor.

"I can't get up, Frances, I just can't."

"That's okay, Pam, we'll think of something else."

In the end they slid her on her backside out of the door to wait for the ambulance so we could carry on eating, though nobody could eat except me. Everyone was silent with their mouths wide open and all that could be heard was me, crunching on an apple. Suki looked at me, disgusted. Eventually the ambulance arrived and invalid was taken to hospital. The kitchen manager came in everyone to tell us what had happened.

"I'm afraid Mrs Norris has broken her ankle in the custard."

Looking back now, it was probably the way she said it. I burst out laughing. Everyone turned to me with hard, stony glares, and none more than Suki.

"It's not funny, Rebekah." I then screamed with laughter even more, knowing that I was annoying Suki. This set us up for an afternoon that is yet to finish.

The afternoon was taken up with English and, because this was Crime Prevention Week, Miss Pike thought it would be a nice idea for us to write poison pen letters. I wondered if she wrote any other kind. I gathered up newspapers and magazines and placed them on the groups' tables along with pots of glue and boxes of scissors. It was probably while I was handing out the scissors that the idea began.

Thinking of something horrible to say was hard work for me, but one look at Suki gave me divine inspiration. I found the words I needed, cut them out and stuck them on my paper. I was quite impressed with my handiwork. As usual I was the first to finish even though I had started last, so I took my criminal achievement up to Miss Pike's desk.

"What is the meaning of this?" she yelled, waving my master-piece in front of my eyes. The whole class sat quietly, staring pensively at me. "Class, I want you all to take a good look at this child and listen very carefully to what she has written." Miss Pike cleared her throat. "Dear X. I hate you. Yours sincerely, Rebekah Doen."

I thought it sounded straight to the point but of course Miss Pike had other ideas. I mean, she would know all about poison pen letters as she probably sent them out at times of bereavement.

"Class, what is wrong with this?"

"Should never put your name on a poison pen letter," shouted one cherub.

"You should never start a poison pen letter with 'Dear'. It's bad manners." called out another treasure.

"Quite right. Do you understand?"

I muttered something which vaguely sounded like 'Yes Miss' but which was actually 'You icicle'. I plodded back to my seat and it was then that it happened, that Suki said it.

"Miss Pike, Rebekah didn't understand as she spent her summer holidays with a retard, a certain spasmo who used to live down her street."

"Well, thank you for telling me, Suki. I'll keep my eye on Rebekah Doen all the more now."

That is what others told me that Miss Pike had said but I didn't catch the words, my attention firmly on more important matters. I picked up a pair of scissors, feeling their cold, metallic hardness in my soft hand, and quietly walked to where Suki was sitting. It was all over in such a flash that I cannot really remember actually doing it, though I do recall saying, "This one's for you, Megan."

Suki's long golden plait was laid over her chair, though no longer connected to her head.

—TWENTY-TWO—

I was taken to see Mrs Temple and left outside her door while Miss Pike rushed back to console the hysterical Suki. Mrs Temple opened the door and my blood froze.

"Nice seeing you again," she said.

I followed her into the room where she turned and knelt down in front of me. "Don't let them rattle you. I don't want to see you turning into a Venus Fly Trap. As for this episode, I'll just think of you as a rose in thorns."

"Doesn't every rose have thorns?"

"Yes, but today someone had definitely been cut by yours." Mrs. Temple smiled and I immediately felt the blood flowing through my veins again. I was alive once more. "Now, what punishment shall I give you?" I looked to the floor.

"I'm sorry, Mrs Temple. I just couldn't help myself. Suki said something nasty about my friend that died."

"That was Megan Doherty?" I nodded in agreement, my eyes still glued to the floor. "Yes, I heard about that, Rebekah." Mrs Temple went to sit in her comfortable rocking chair. It was not behind the desk but in a corner; next to it stood her guitar and on the other side was a huge plant with thick green leaves.

All I answered was, "I dived in after her, Mrs Temple. I tried to save her."

I glanced up at her rocking in the chair, her arms opened to me. I swallowed some tears down and walked silently, very slowly, to Mrs Temple's arms. She sat me on her knee and rocked me gently.

"This is some detention, eh?"

"It's just right for the crime."

"Mmm, I wonder what Miss Pike would say?"

"Oh, I don't even want to think about her." I held Mrs Temple close to me. She smelled of roses and marzipan.

"Do you think I should change and become stricter like Miss Pike?"

"No. Whatever for?"

"Well, I am the Headmistress after all."

"Well, yes, you are. But you are a Headmistress for a reason and that reason is now. Miss Pike is a teacher and I suppose if I'm honest she has a reason too."

Mrs Temple stopped rocking and tilted her head to look at me.

"You know, Becky, you really are mature for your age."

"What's mature, Mrs Temple?"

"You have a lot of wisdom. It's almost as if you've been through all this before."

"Ha! I don't think I could have lived through this twice."

Mrs Temple continued to rock and I rested my head on her breast once more. It was uncomplicated. It was true. It was honest. It was warm. It was simple. It was just caring for another human being. And it was just being there. We sat rocking, not talking, just rocking to and fro, to and fro, encased in our own thoughts but safe in the knowledge that we had each other to talk to if we wanted to. But the silence was understood, just as it had been with Megan.

Suffice to say, detention came to an end far too quickly for my liking and soon the hour was over. Mrs Temple stopped rocking.

"Well, Becky, it looks like your detention is over."

"Aye, it was really hard," I joked as I clambered off her knee.

"Yes, I hope my punishment has shown you that crime doesn't pay." We both laughed. She got up from the rocking chair, straightened her skirt and walked to the door which she opened for me. "I hope I don't see you in here for detention again too soon."

"I'll miss it, but I'll try and be good for your sake, Mrs Temple."

"Oh no, Becky, if you must do something it is always for yourself."

"But isn't that selfish?"

"Becky, after all is said and done it is you who must live with yourself and no-one else. So don't pay any attention to anyone, just you, okay?"

"Alright. Thank you, Mrs Temple. See ya."

"See you, Becky. And be good."

As I walked past my classroom I could see Suki there with her mother, Miss Pike hovering over them. Suki's mother was more hysterical than her daughter and was trying to stick the hair back on with sellotape and glue.

"Oh Jan, what are we going to do?" Suki's mother knew Miss Pike by her first name, so there was indeed no hope for Suki or her mother.

If anyone had seen me walk home that evening, they may have said the same about me. I was not well. The events of the day had left me feeling very sick.

The shadow swooped over me.

Am I here? Am I real? I feel as though I'm in a dream. Yet I feel the air upon my face and see my face reflected back to me in the eyes of people I walk past. I feel the chill of the town. I breathe the air yet seem to be floating. I seem to be living on a hope, a fragile, thin and weak chance. My head feels fuzzy. It feels heavy. Every leaf that trembles in the sun sets me back to where I began. Am I here now?

I am standing in quiet solitude, wondering where I'm going and where I've been. I am all alone with thoughts, no words, just empty thoughts without a rhyme echoing round my mind. I found myself at home but had no idea how I got there. Mother saw me as I came in.

"Oh my God! What's happened? You look terrible. We'd better get you upstairs."

"No, don't touch me. I can manage." I shook my hands with frustration. I turned round, round and round again in the living room not knowing which direction to go in. Then I realised I was moving, being guided up the stairs. Peter was in front and mother held me behind in case I fell backwards. Leah had opened the bedroom door.

"Here you are, then. Let's get your shoes off."

"No! I can do it myself."

Mother stood back. Peter had disappeared downstairs while Leah hovered in the corner with my pyjamas.

I tried to take my shoes off but my hands kept misjudging where my feet were and I missed them each time. I fell on the bed exhausted and lay unmoving as I felt my shoes being taken off my feet. I was too tired to speak. Leah and our mother worked in silence as they got me ready for bed. I didn't go to school for a week, and I can't remember that week either.

The next few weeks heralded a new beginning for me. Cutting Suki's hair was a symbol of revenge. Miss Pike had become unsure of how to deal with this rather sneaky Irish rebel. So most days I became a table all on my own, too black for the Black Team.

Unfortunately for Miss Pike, she put me in the furthest place from the rest of the class, which happened to be near the window.

I stared out of the window as I had done so many times before. But this time I felt different. I had come full circle. The spring was ending and another summer beginning. I felt the earth changing. The buds on the trees were bursting open and new green life was beginning its cycle. The grass on the sports field looked so green I could almost smell its freshness through the glass of the window. I wanted so badly to be free to go outside.

Miss Pike relished her morning ritual of tormenting her class with the government's directive of giving milk to children. I sat holding my bottle and longing to be outside with the rest of the school. Mrs Temple was there and the other children gathered round her like honey bees to the queen. They were drawn to her, perhaps by the colours she wore, perhaps by her nature that shone through, her eyes saying 'You can trust me'. Or perhaps it was the fact that she believed everyone had some good in them, no matter what you had done in the past. No matter what had happened, she believed that everyone deserved a chance to prove themselves. There was no badness in a child, no 'evil manifest', only misguided imagination and the need for attention.

Mrs Temple had chosen playground duty herself to see if she could stop the bullying of certain children i.e. me. As she walked round the playground with half the school holding onto her and following her, she noticed me looking out of the window. Miss Pike had her back to us, scrubbing the blackboard.

Mrs Temple came over to our classroom window, winked at me and tapped on the glass with her blue painted nails.

"Miss Doen, I will kindly remind you not to tap on windows."

"But - "

"What have I told you about 'buts', Miss Doen?" The bitch turned round to see Mrs Temple pulling faces at her through the glass.

"It wasn't me, Miss Pike. It was the Headmistress, Mrs Temple."

Miss Pike rubbed her hands together. "I'm quite aware who the Headmistress is, thank you, Rebekah Doen," Miss Pike declared as she walked to the window. The whole class was silent as we waited to see the outcome. Miss Pike opened the window where Mrs Temple stood smiling, pulling faces and giggling at her. You could hear a pin drop. Then all of a sudden:

"Hello, Miss Pike! What a glorious day. Why isn't your class out here enjoying the beautiful sun?"

"They're having their milk."

"What? Well, why don't they have it before playtime?"

"That would mean partaking of it in lesson time. You would not wish the pupils to miss out on their lessons now, Mrs Temple?"

"No, of course not, Miss Pike. But on days such as this our children should be out getting fresh air into their lungs." Mrs Temple strained her neck to look round the classroom. "Has everyone finished their milk?"

No-one answered, for although Mrs Temple was Headmistress of the entire school, the boss, we knew she was not our teacher; and our teacher had not asked the question. Miss Pike looked round her class and answered for us. "It appears that most of the pupils have indeed finished their milk, Mrs Temple."

"Good. Good. Well, that's final then. Come on you lot, get your skates on. You don't want to waste any more playtime."

We did not move. Miss Pike stood firm with her hands tightly clasped together. Then, "You may proceed as the Headmistress advised."

The whole class jumped out of their chairs and scrambled from the classroom. As I left, I overheard Mrs Temple tease Miss Pike, saying, "Well, they were really in a hurry to get out of your class, weren't they, Miss Pike? Was it another poison pen letter lesson?" I didn't hear Miss Pike's reply.

I bounded outside. I felt so strong. Mrs Temple was bombarded with more eager children and waded round the playground knee deep in them. She saw me and began to steer the gang my way.

"Now then, Rebekah, did we enjoy our milk?" She winked at me.

I smiled. "Aye, it was alright."

"Good. Good."

The air tasted sweet. The birds were singing. Children were playing. The smell of fresh flowers and grass mowed for the first time since the long winter surrounded me as I gazed up into the sky.

"Isn't it a glorious day, Rebekah?"

"Aye, Mrs Temple, really brilliant."

I took a deep breath of this spring air and felt its energy flood my lungs with strength. My body felt powerful. I could feel the very toes in my shoes as they moved and stretched, wanting to be put to some good use. I glanced at Mrs Temple's shoes. "They're smart shoes, Mrs Temple."

"Why, thank you, Rebekah. They're my magic shoes, they can take me anywhere."

"Really, Miss?" said one of the little cherubs hanging onto her.

"No, not really, Andrew. But they're so comfortable I can walk anywhere in them."

I bit my lip. "Can you run in them, Mrs Temple?"

She studied me, knowing what I was thinking. "Yes, Rebekah, as a matter of fact I can run in them. Why?"

"Well, Mrs Temple, would you like a race?"

"A race?"

"Yes, a race between you and me."

She rolled her eyes. "Well, I don't know... maybe... oh, go on then. Yeah, I'd love a race with you, Rebekah." The cherubs hanging onto her gasped. "Come on, let's go to the field and run." Mrs Temple tried to move towards the school field but a dozen children still held on fast to her. "Now children, you heard Rebekah, we're going to have a race. So you're going to have to let me go. Okay?"

"But Miss…" came the cries. At last the children let go with pleas and sighs.

Mrs Temple skipped free onto the school field and I strolled across to where she was loosening up, shaking her hands, arms, legs and feet. She moved her head from side to side as a crowd began to gather. She turned to me.

"How far do you want to run, Becky?"

"Forever."

Her eyes met mine and searched deep within them, then she smiled. "Not today, dear. Got to do the shopping tonight. How about to the end of the field and back again?"

"Aye, that sounds far enough for today. Are you sure you want to run against me today, Mrs Temple?"

"Yes. Yes, indeed. It's such a marvellously glorious day. I'm full of life and exuberance and…"

"Strength?"

"Yes. You feel it too, eh? Well well. That's good."

By now the whole school had gathered round the sports field, indeed even Miss Pike and other teachers had boldly ventured outside. This was something unheard of at Break time but they were as curious as everyone. Jack the Caretaker looked like he was taking bets; after my disastrous Sports Day event of last summer, I'm sure the odds were on me losing. But this day was different. I felt stronger than I had ever been before. I could feel the power of the coming summer surging through my veins. The sun's power raced through my muscles and bones, making me feel invincible.

Liza had wangled a front row view. "What are you doing?"

"What does it look like? I'm going to race Mrs Temple."

"Why?"

"'Cause I want to."

"You're mad. She'll win."

"Well, thank you, Liza, for that vote of confidence."

"Becky, just think back to last summer. The only reason why you - "

"I do think back to last summer, Liza. I never stop thinking about last summer."

"What happens if you get ill while you're running and have a dizzy spell?"

"Liza?"

"Yes?"

"Shut up." She skulked back into the audience.

"Right then, Miss Doen. Are you ready?"

"Aye, Miss."

"Good. All you in the first row, I want you to count down from three. Do you understand? And when you get to one, shout GO, okay? So it's 3 – 2 – 1 – GO. Alright?"

There was a chorus of "Yes, Mrs Temple" synchronised with nodding heads.

I stood next to Mrs Temple. She leaned forward, her face full of eager anticipation. "Good luck, Mrs Temple."

"You too, Becky. May the best man win!" She smiled back at me, then gave a nod to the countdown masters to her left. Her arms were already up as if to run, her fists clenched tightly. She would enjoy this even more than me.

"3 – 2 – 1 – GO!" shouted out the entire school, deafening both of us. I looked towards Mrs Temple but she'd already gone, bouncing into the race like a kangaroo. I leaped forward and felt as though the air were carrying me across the field. I caught her up in no time and flowed right past her as she bounced up and down on the field. Her legs flew upwards as she ran and her knees looked like they were going to hit her chin, she raised them so much, and her arms were out of sync with the rest of her. But still she gave her everything.

The fence loomed closer and I ran into it first, the force pushing me back into the race, and as we returned I was in the lead. I ran past the entire school. I could see teachers and children shouting with fists thumping the air, but I could not hear a word. The world was silent, the way it had been the night Auntie Maggie, Megan and I had run away, only to find ourselves at the end of the pier.

It all made perfect sense. I had been running for as long as I could remember. I was free.

I could see the line and put my arms out as if to break through to the other side. I had no idea how far Mrs Temple was behind me. The people standing at the front signalled me to slow down, but I couldn't. They could see me coming closer and closer towards them at full speed, so they moved out of the way and I kept on running. As I broke through them, I finally heard their applause and cheers.

—TWENTY-THREE—

The sound of doors slamming and my mother crying behind them is one of the familiar memories I have of childhood. The other is Megan.

Mrs Doherty returned to Ireland but her beloved daughter was buried in an English cemetery. I learned later that the funeral had been a quiet affair, stillness echoing round the church. Megan's mother sat the entire time. People say she could not move and her eyes never left the sight of her daughter's coffin. The church was empty except for Mrs Doherty, my mother, Liza and her mother. Father didn't go to the funeral. It seems strange that it was only women who paid their respects to an eternal child and understood one another's pain. No-one cried, their faces testimony to so many years of heartache as another innocent was laid in the arms of a painted Virgin Mary.

While I lay in bed tortured by what I had seen, not sure of where my soul wanted to be, my friend was committed to the earth forever. And Auntie Maggie was committed again too, by father.

Liza had a problem dealing with the death of a friend and the illness of another who had survived. So, in their fear, Liza's parents took her and her brothers away on holiday for the very first time. For the six weeks of the summer Liza spent only one week in the town and then she was off visiting grandparents and doing 'other stuff'. Anything rather than be with me.

I did not want the attention of an overpowering mother, intent on proving doctors wrong. In my frustration, I knew that the time of a school holiday could be better used. I wanted to find the cemetery and to see Megan again. I didn't really know what I would find there as I had never been to a cemetery before. And I had no idea where it was, so I decided to ask Leah.

"What do you want to know for?"

"I just do. Do you know where it is?"

She went quiet and her chin rested on her chest as she gazed at the floor. "Why, Becky?" she whispered.

"I think you know why, Leah."

"I think I do. But I don't understand why you would want to. She's not there."

"What do you mean?"

"Well, her coffin's there and that but you know her soul's in Heaven now."

"Leah?"

"Yes?"

"Just stop with the mass. Or do you want me to get you some candles?"

"Oh, Becky, I'm just trying…"

"I know what you're doing but I don't want to hear it. Just tell me where the bloody cemetery is."

"Alright. Look, I'll come with you."

"No. I need to do this on my own."

"But you might get lost or ill. It's a fair old distance, you know."

"No, Leah. Thank you, but I need to do this on my own. I need to say goodbye by myself. Tell me the easiest way. Please?"

"Okay. But for Christ's sake don't let Mammy know I told you, okay?"

"Okay."

"She doesn't want you going. She thinks it'll upset you."

"Upset me?" I laughed. "Upset me! What in Hell could possibly upset me now after everything I've fucking been through?"

"Oh Becky, your language."

"Well honestly, what bloody planet is that woman living on, for Christ's sake?"

"She just worries about you."

"Well, she didn't worry about me a year ago, did she?"

Leah winced, she'd been hurt. It had been thrown in her face. We had all danced around it. We had walked on eggshells of lies and now it was all shattering into minute pieces.

"Give her a chance, Becky."

"Like she did me?"

"What's happened to you lately? You're so bloody angry."

"Nothing, Leah. It's just… it's just…"

"What?"

"Life's too short for this kind of shit. Now, are you gonna tell me where that damn cemetery is?"

My poor sister stood gob smacked and in her shock told me the easiest way, for me to remember that is, to get to the cemetery. I had to go through the park and keep walking until I came to the main road and then follow the signs. I had to keep looking for them just in case I did get lost. Before I set out, Leah made sure I had some money in my pocket. She broke into her piggy bank and gave me what was left of her pocket money, just to `phone home if I did get lost. I was adamant I wouldn't need it but she insisted I take it.

She also insisted that she would walk with me to the park, saying it would look good if we left the house together so mother wouldn't get suspicious and wonder where I was going. Yet Leah had another reason to walk with me to the park - she was meeting Mark, the scrawny boy with dirty blond hair.

All went according to plan and mother didn't suspect a thing. Indeed, she called after us both to take our coats as it looked like rain. As we approached the park I could see Mark, his hands stuffed firmly into his kagool pockets and his hair falling into his eyes. He kicked the ground in anticipation and Leah giggled.

"Ooo! There he is. He's waiting for me."

I thought I'd be sick.

"Hi, Mark."

"Yeah. Hi, Leah." They stood for what felt like an hour just staring at the floor and then quickly glancing at one another before looking away again.

"I'm Becky."

"Oh yeah, this is Becky, Mark, my little sister."

"Yeah. Hi, little sister Becky." Silence again while their eyes played games of catch-me-if-you-can with one another.

"Well, I'd love to stay and chat but I really must be going."

"Yeah. Okay."

"You do remember the way, don't you? You haven't forgotten? And you've got that money just in case?"

"Yes."

"Are you sure?"

"Yes."

"Alright. Take care, Becky."

"Yes. Take care, Leah. See ya later. See ya later, Mark."

"Yeah. See ya, little sister Becky."

I left them there, the two lovebirds at the gates, while I walked on into the open field of the park. Trees lined the path and here and there were flowerbeds of dying daffodils and the first fresh roses of the summer. Across the field in the sky darted a swallow, diving in and out of imaginary waves as the air currents flowed.

The sky was now heavy and overcast but I walked on. I did not feel well. I watched the swallow dart up and down once more, dancing through the air for the summer. Yet one swallow does not make a summer. Then suddenly they darted in front of me, hundreds of swallows dancing before me. What was happening? Thoughts and ideas spun round in my head, making me feel dizzy even though I was lying down in bed. In bed? What was I doing in bed? I was in the park…

Each time the shadow swept over me I felt as though I would die. Indeed, I think a piece of me probably did, because looking back now I feel nothing for those who were so afraid of me. I saw Katie and Suki dancing in and out of the air with the swallows. What was happening?

"What?"

"Shhh, Becky, it's alright. It's over now."

The rain pelted down, buffeted by the wind. It tapped on the glass like apprehensive fingernails, anxious for a new summer.

"What's that?"

"It's the rain."

"Rain?"

"Aye, it didn't half rain, a real cloudburst. Luckily, we just got in before it really pelted down."

"What happened, Leah? We were in the park."

"Well, when you said goodbye and walked on into the park, then it began to rain. I was worried that you were gonna get soaked. So Mark thought it best we go after you and tell you to wait under the shelter with us. You remember Mark, don't you?"

"The man of many words."

"Yeah. He's so caring, I - "

"Leah!"

"Oh, yeah. Right, so we walked after you and then we saw you just standing in the middle of the field not doing anything, just staring. There was this flash of lightning and we knew it was really gonna chuck it down. I don't know whether you could hear us or not, but we walked back home with you. Mark made sure you were okay. Isn't he considerate?"

"Leah!"

"Mmm…"

"I don't remember it at all. I don't remember walking home."

"Becky?"

"I don't like that. I don't like not knowing. I want to remember everything."

"Can't you remember anything?"

"No, not about walking home, only the swallows."

"The swallows? Don't you remember the rainbow? You were muttering about the rainbow."

"No, I only saw swallows darting up and down. That's what I was looking at."

"We didn't see that, just you standing motionless and staring at the sky. We thought you were staring at the rainbow."

"I did see that."

"Well, the swallows were probably gone by the time we got there. The flash of lightning probably scared them away."

"Aye, that's right."

No more was said between us two sisters. We never talked any more about the swallows. It was one of those moments in my childhood that the family has cleared away into the closet along with the other embarrassing moments.

Leah knew that I would still want to go the cemetery. My desire had not yet dissolved in submission to mother's overprotective reaches. I was determined to find Megan, so once again my sister smuggled us out of the house with the story that we were going to the park for some fresh air. It was only half a lie; our consciences were clear and what mother didn't know wouldn't hurt her. This time Leah, and Mark for that matter, walked with me through the park and onwards to the main road where a huge sign for the cemetery loomed above us.

"Look, if you follow that you'll have no problems, alright?"

"Aye, alright, Leah."

"You've got that money anyway. But we'll waiting in the park for you anyway. Alright Mark?"

"Yeah."

"Look, you don't have to wait for me. I don't know how long I'm gonna be, Leah."

"It's alright, Becky. We'll be there."

"Okay. See you, Leah, and thanks. See you, Mark."

"Yeah! Right. See ya."

Once more I left Leah and Mark and walked on alone, following the signs to the cemetery. This time I'd set out knowing that I'd find the cemetery but I didn't know for sure if I'd find Megan. Yet the cemetery held some kind of fascination for me and, when at last I found it, I knew why. The huge stone gates stood majestic and proud, heralding the last journey of the body. I walked through into the vast stillness of peace, amazed at the sight that befell me: hundreds and hundreds of headstones of all different shapes and sizes, laid out over the land as far as the eye could see. No wonder the cemetery was on the outskirts of town - there was no room for the dead where the living were concerned.

Yet I had to find Megan. I walked through the rows looking at names, glancing at tombs, wondering who was buried where there were no names, just weeds and centuries' old amnesia of dead relatives. Trees lined paths that ran off in different directions with secluded corners of yet more graves. I came to a huge section of white crosses, rows and rows of them taking up all that particular part of the graveyard. I turned down one of the little paths away from the crosses; some of the graves here had fresh earth over their rounded hills and wreaths of flowers going brown on top of them.

I wanted to find Megan so much, to see where they had placed her. I asked over and over in my mind, "Megan, where are you? Help me find you. Please tell me where you are." But I couldn't find her. I searched and searched. I went down all the little paths. I tore away plants from headstones to see if she was there. But I couldn't find her anywhere. The evening was coming and as the sun slowly set I began my walk home. I had lost her again. Yet although I had not forgotten my way home, I had forgotten the way out of the cemetery...

In the distance, I could see the row of white crosses and I knew the entrance was somewhere past there, so I headed towards them. And just as I was turning down towards the main entrance, something made me turn my head to the side and there she was. I had found her. I had found Megan. I walked slowly towards the grave, reading the headstone's words as they came closer:

Megan Doherty
Beloved daughter of Mary Doherty and dearly missed Patrick.
Father and daughter together among the angels.
R.I.P.

I fell to my knees. Something inside seemed to snap and I just broke. My heart split in two. I cried, uncontrollably. The shadow came over me many times there but every time I came round I was still crying; even the shadow couldn't stop my tears.

'Why didn't you hold my hand? I wouldn't have let you fall. Auntie could have pulled us both up. Oh Megan, I hold your hand and watch you slip away but I don't want you to. Stay. Stay with me and play. I'll play all the games you want to. Please just stay.'

It was over. I stared at the grave and wondered if Megan was warm enough.

'I don't think you like it in there. You never liked the dark, did you, Megan? You can't see your rainbows in there. I'll miss you, my friend. I'll never forget you, Megan. Thank you for being you. Goodbye, good friend.'

As I walked away, the tears burned my eyes; they gushed down my cheeks and I felt their heat. I walked slowly down the path. I saw for the very first time the beauty of the tall trees that had stood to attention since the beginning. The trees were alive and breathing, their arms reaching out with fluttering leaves dancing from them. The sun bounced in between the dancing leaves and I listened for the music. At last I heard it. I stood there underneath the trees, watching the dancing leaves weaving in and out the rays of the sun, in and out, softly, softly, breathing in and out

I closed my eyes and could still feel the dance of the leaves upon my mind. When I opened my eyes, the rays of the sun still weaved between the leaves. It was summer and their dance had yet to finish. Mine had yet to begin. I closed my eyes and again breathed in the soft silence of the dance. I opened them once more and suddenly, silently, it swooped down upon me. Blackness surrounded me and I could no longer feel the dance, no longer smell the freshness of the shadows cast by the trees I stood under, no longer hear their leaves rustling like a waterfall.

I could not see. I could not feel. I could not hear. I could not smell. I was not there.

I followed the signs, this time to the park, and as I walked closer to it I could see Leah and Mark standing where they had left me, what seemed like years ago.

"Are you alright? We were getting worried. Did you get lost?"

"Yes, I'm alright and no, I didn't get lost."

"Good. Well, it's getting late. We'd better get off home or Mammy will have us both."

"Aye."

Leah took one hand, Mark took the other, and I walked home between them. As I walked along the street, the haunted house loomed closer but it no longer held any mystery. The avenue's foreboding haunt was no longer the secret on everyone's tongue. Megan's house was up for sale. A large white board stuck on a stick in the ground with a For Sale notice dominated Mrs Doherty's beloved garden.

There was still warmth in the sun and the gentle breeze was kind, yet it had a chill within it that penetrated my heart as I walked along the so familiar street. Somehow, the life had gone out of it. It no longer sparkled with children playing their games of imagination, games which I had once been a part of but could no longer join in. Megan had gone and my heart wore a heavy load. I prayed that I had not taken her for granted, though deep down I knew that I had. She had been everything to me - the sister I never talked to, the brother I never played with, the mother I never held and the father I could never look up to.

In the years that followed, I would work with those who have Down syndrome. A colleague once raised the point that such people have an extra chromosome and she couldn't understand why, as a result, they were not super-intelligent. The answer is clear to me, and it is not about intelligence. If we have an extra chromosome, the result is that it makes us extra sensitive, with heightened emotions. We love more than the average person. We feel more and our hearts are more developed. To be human is to love and an extra chromosome enhances our ability to love.

I knew that this feeling would be with me always. A feeling such as this does not fade and die but is carried within, and I knew it would return to haunt me at times of great sadness. It is a feeling of such sadness and complete emptiness that one would almost give life itself for everlasting peace.

Yet there was something that would hold me back from that, something so strong that I could never really fight it. And in my moments of greatest blackness it would come just in time to save me from becoming sane in this insane world.

I think back to the rainbows and the storms of that year. I see rainbows now and it all pours back.

I look at a rainbow and think…

Christ Jesus! I survived and I am still here!

IF YOU HAVE ENJOYED THIS BOOK…

Local Legend is committed to publishing the very best spiritual writing, both fiction and non-fiction. You might also enjoy:

A SINGLE PETAL
Oliver Eade (ISBN 978-1-907203-42-8)

Winner of the national Local Legend Spiritual Writing Competition, this page-turner is a novel of murder, politics and passion set in ancient China. Yet its themes of loyalty, commitment and deep personal love are every bit as relevant for us today as they were in past times. The author is an expert on Chinese culture and history, and his debut adult novel deserves to become a classic.

AURA CHILD
A I Kaymen (ISBN 978-1-907203-71-8)

One of the most astonishing books ever written, telling the true story of a genuine Indigo child. Genevieve grew up in a normal London family but from an early age realised that she had very special spiritual and psychic gifts. She saw the energy fields around living things, read people's thoughts and even found herself slipping through time, able to converse with the spirits of those who had lived in her neighbourhood. This is an uplifting and inspiring book for what it tells us about the nature of our minds.

CELESTIAL AMBULANCE
Ann Matkins (ISBN 978-1-907203-45-9)

A brave and delightful comedy novel. Having died of cancer, Ben wakes up in the afterlife looking forward to a good rest, only to find that everyone is expected to get a job! He becomes the driver of an ambulance (with a mind of her own), rescuing the spirits of others who have died suddenly and delivering them safely home. This book is as thought-provoking as it is entertaining.

THE QUIRKY MEDIUM
Alison Wynne-Ryder (ISBN 978-1-907203-47-3)

Alison is the co-host of the TV show *Rescue Mediums*, in which she puts herself in real danger to free homes of lost and often malicious spirits. Yet she is a most reluctant medium, afraid of ghosts! This is her amazing and often very funny autobiography, taking us 'back stage' of the television production as well as describing how she came to discover the psychic gifts that have brought her an international following.

5P1R1T R3V3L4T10N5
Nigel Peace (ISBN 978-1-907203-14-5)

With descriptions of more than a hundred proven prophetic dreams and many more everyday synchronicities, the author shows us that, without doubt, we can know the future and that everyone can receive genuine spiritual guidance for our lives' challenges. World-renowned biologist Dr Rupert Sheldrake has endorsed this book as "...vivid and fascinating... pioneering research..."

SIMPLY SPIRITUAL
Jacqui Rogers (ISBN 978-1-907203-75-6)

The 'spookies' started contacting Jacqui when she was a child and never gave up until, at last, she developed her psychic talents and became the successful international medium she is now. This is a moving account of her difficult life and her triumph over adversity, with many great stories of her spiritual readings.

Further details and extracts of these and many
other beautiful titles may be seen at
www.local-legend.co.uk

FURTHER INFORMATION

If you have been affected by the issues raised in this book and would like further advice, there are several societies offering help:

Epilepsy
Epilepsy Action - *www.epilepsy.org.uk*
The Epilepsy Society - *www.epilepsysociety.org.uk*
UK Epilepsy - *www.ukepilepsy.com*

Down Syndrome
Amy's House - *www.amyshouse.org.uk*
National Down Syndrome Society (New York) - *www.ndss.org*
Down Syndrome Association - *www.downs-syndrome.org.uk*
Down Syndrome Education International - *www.dseinternational.org*

Others
Mental Health Foundation - *www.mhf.org.uk*
British Society for Mental Health and Deafness - *www.bsmhd.org.uk*
The British Psychological Society - *www.bps.org.uk*
MIND - *www.mind.org.uk*
Mencap - *www.mencap.org.uk*

Lightning Source UK Ltd.
Milton Keynes UK
UKOW07f0328021214

242488UK00018BA/930/P